## UBER HEROES & B1

A new age of heroes began in 2006 with the appearance of Earth's first beta human – Dr. Nemesis, endowed with the might of a living titan. Next was the Flame, who possessed the ability to create and control fire. Then came the Crusader in 2007, the first uberhero, a costumed vigilante who fought crime. In 2019, a small group of these uberheroes banded together to form the Guild.

In 2023, its members are Black Fury, the Blazing Scarab, Cerebex, the Crusader, Dr. Nemesis, Dynamic Man, the Fighting Yank, the Flame, Jinx, Kitten, and Magno.

OTHER WESTERNTAINMENT BOOKS

*The Adventures of the Man of Bronze: a Definitive Chronology* (3rd ed.) by Jeff Deischer

*The Way They Were*
by Jeff Deischer
*v1: The Victorian Age*
*v2: The Pulp Era*
*v3: Action Heroes*

WORLDS COLLIDE
by Jeff Deischer
*Beyond Worlds Collide*
*War of Worlds Collide*
*Under Worlds Collide*

THE GOLDEN AGE
by Jeff Deischer
*Mystico*
*Dark of the Moon*
*The Golden Age*
*Future Tense*
*Bad Moon Rising*

THE STEEL RING
by R. A. Jones
*The Steel Ring*
*The Twilight War*
*The House of Souls*
*A Ring of Worlds*

THE HERITAGE UNIVERSE by Jeff Deischer
*Hide and Seek*
*Tag, You Are It!*
*Duck Duck Goose*
*War!*
*Peek-a-Boo*
*Toy Soldiers*

*Inner Space*
*Split Decision*
*Next Generation, part 1*
*Next Generation, part 2*
*New World Order*

DOC BRAZEN
by Jeff Deischer
*Millennium Bug*
*Dead Wrong*
*Net Prophet*
*Acid Test*
*Infernal Machine*
*Golden Opportunity*
*Talking Heads*
*Element of Surprise*
*Wild Life*

NEMESIS COMPANY
by Jeff Deischer
*The Secret of the ...*
*Suicidal Sparrow*
*Red, as in Ruin*
*Sky Terror*
*The World-Shakers*
*The Yesterday Menace*

# THE DAY AFTER

# TOMORROW

Jeff Deischer

a **WESTERNTAINMENT** publication

THE DAY AFTER TOMORROW
published by Westerntainment
Denver, Colorado, USA
HTTP://Westerntainment.blogspot.com
westerntainment@gmail.com

*The Day After Tomorrow* copyright 2023 Jeff Deischer

No part of this publication may be reprinted without permission, except for purposes of review or scholarly discussion. All rights reserved.

Dedicated to the memory of

Murray Ward, my best friend, soul mate,
and the best proofreader a writer could ask for

# Acknowledgments

Thanks to:

The Fulton Street Irregulars: David Webb, Mark Marderosian, and Peter Garcia for their valuable feedback;

Wikipedia, without which my books could not be written;

The Public Domain Super Heroes wiki;

And my father, for his support.

Foreword

## THESE ARE NOT YOUR GREAT-GRANDFATHER'S SUPERHEROES

This is not the first time I've used public domain superheroes. It's in fact the fifth *series* of my PD work, though two of the earlier series, THE SENSATIONAL SENTINELS and HERO U.N.I.O.N., belong to the same universe, my Heritage Universe, which takes the PD(ish) heroes of the mid or late Sixties and groups them in the same universe. This includes Charlton, Tower, Dell, and M. F. Enterprises characters in (thus far) eleven volumes.

The first time I used public domain heroes in a project was back in the early or mid Eighties. I didn't know they were in the public domain. I didn't even know what that *was* at the time.

I had one of those comic book price guides, and I was fascinated by the names of all these superheroes I'd never heard of. So I created a bunch of characters based solely on what these names suggested to me. I don't know what happened to that project, how far along I got – but it wasn't very far. I've decided to try this concept again in this book, pairing it with a new style of writing for me. But I've reversed the process here, starting with a personality or origin or super, ahem, *uber* powers, then finding a name or ability to go with it. In most cases, origins were the last piece of the character puzzle.

I've written a lot of superhero books – more than

anyone else on the *planet*, in fact: 33 as I write this to be precise (28 have been published). In most of these I used public domain characters, or PD-adjacent ones, which are either orphan characters who are not in PD but no one caring what becomes of them, so are ripe for use; and pastiches I've created when part of a defunct characters are in PD and others are not (such as Charlton; DC bought only part of their stable of superheroes, primarily the popular "action heroes" – which they proceeded to drastically change so they could trademark them); or pastiches when a status is in question or complicated, and I'd rather not get a headache over their status. To the best of my knowledge, I've never used a character which was illegal to publish a story using him or her.

I started using public domain characters with my THE GOLDEN AGE series in 2012 because I thought it would be good exposure. I was still a novice author who'd had only six novels – only one a superhero book that wasn't selling – published at the time, and I thought familiar or semi-familiar characters might help attract attention in the superhero prose world (I seem to be the second person to write and publish a superhero prose novel, after Bobby Nash). A big attraction for me as a writer is – and I suspect *others* who work with PD characters – these characters have backgrounds upon which to draw: villains and supporting cast and milieu. These of course can be used whole cloth, but for me, at least, it's inspirational for story ideas and character development. Like modern readers, I like some meat on the bones of golden age characters, superhero and otherwise.

So while this is not my first use of PD superheroes, it is my first using this *style of writing* for them. It is in fact my *fourth* try at a story like this, using the hard third POV for superheroes, in which readers only know about characters from what the characters say and do. This is like film or TV. There are no inner monologues, no "head hopping" (as is the case in comic books – or at least *was* the case when I was reading them decades ago), no memories flooding into the mind of anyone. This style is best known in detective stories, where the air of mystery makes everyone a suspect.

I've taken all I've learned in the writing of my 33 superhero books (almost all of them in three multi-volume series) and put it into this novel to try this new style – which I know from earlier attempts is not easy for me.

I hope you enjoy it.


Jeff Deischer
June 2023

P.S. I have been known to rail against retconning characters, altering their genders, sexuality, and/or race or ethnic background for purposes of political correctness as both Marvel and DC have done in their cinematic universes and comic books. That's not taking a moral stand for equality. At best, it's virtue signaling, and at worst, crass commercialism.

And I'm a writer. When I design a character, I take all those aspects into consideration. I've written females, gays/lesbians, Hispanics, blacks, Asians, Muslims, etc. My characters are the way I want them. I don't want some asshole coming along in twenty or thirty years thinking he knows better than I what makes my characters work.

But I support *rebooting* of characters, such as the new all-black THE WONDER YEARS show. This takes nothing away from the original show, and explores a different POV of the same subject matter. I feel the same principle applies here: These are not your great-grandfather's superheroes. Those still exist just as they did eighty years ago. My characters are not even *updated* versions of those heroes, sharing only a codename with them. The costumes, powers, civilian guises, etc. are completely different – a complete reboot.

# THE DAY

# AFTER

# TOMORROW

## Chapter 1

## THE ETERNAL CITY

August 15, 2023
Kyoto, Japan

Small peanut-hued men in burnt orange-colored robes led the tall, bony Caucasian and his team of laborers along an underground passage lit only by torches. The flashlight brought by the foreigner remained unused. The passage was narrow and roughhewn, having been carved by primitive tools. The group had left a natural cave behind them some time, and some altitude, ago.

A local Japanese interpreter translated what was being said by the monks of Mount Hiei just outside of Kyoto as they walked. Thought to have originally been the domain of gods and demons in Shinto lore, Mount Hiei was home to the Temple of Enryaku-ji, the first outpost of Japanese Tendai Buddhism, built in 788 by Saicho, who had started the sect after a visit to China. He had also brought tea from China to Japan according to tradition. The compound consisted of the West Pagoda Saito near the summit; the East Pagoda Todo, where the temple had been founded near the summit; and Yokawa, a remote area in the northern section of the area that was less well developed. The temple had become something of a tourist attraction in the last century.

## 2

Due to its location northeast of Kyoto, the previous capital of Japan for over a thousand years, Mount Hiei was believed in geomancy terms to protect the city from the supernatural. The monks believed this even now. One who was named Nho – he was aged but not the oldest of the monks – said as the small group arrived at a small crack in the wall at the end of the passage: "We have not attempted to venture into the new cavern, for fear it would collapse upon us. We are not engineers."

Alex Grey, the Westerner, surveyed the opening. It was short and narrow, permitting no more than a small man or a boy to pass through it. He said in a British accent, "This is amazing. It looks as though this wear is new. There is fresh debris at our feet." "Fresh" in archaeological terms meant something different than a layperson would conclude. The rubble was probably no less than a century old. "And you say you had no idea it's been here all this time?"

"Yes, no idea," Nho, the lead monk, assured the archaeologist. "There is no mention of it in our records, so it has not been used for many centuries, at least. Brother Nakamura found it while mapping the cave system under the temple."

After Grey's interpreter had translated, the archaeologist said, "What do you think is in it?"

"We do not know," answered Nho. "But since it is undoubtedly old, we require the services of an archaeologist who knows how to explore without destroying, and how to preserve antiquities. This cavern may hold artifacts from the early days of Tendai."

Grey saw what Nho was talking about. The small opening appeared fragile looking. He said, "It should be no problem to shore this up, and enlarge the opening safely. And then we'll see what lies inside."

"*Hai*," Nho said with a nod of his head.

The Englishman knew enough Japanese to understand this meant "good".

With this approval, the foreigners went to work.

Grey's team had not done much digging – they were very careful, as the monks watched over their efforts, doing a preliminary inspection – when they uncovered a plaque just inside the opening. It appeared under the illumination of a flashlight that the cavern widened considerably just beyond the opening. The shape seemed to resemble that of a bottle, wide with a narrow neck. The end of some sort of slab was just tantalizingly visible on the other side. It suggested a sarcophagus, which the Japanese did not use, or perhaps an altar, which was more likely.

The plaque was made of stone, with raised characters on it. Grey's native translator announced, "I cannot read it." The Japanese written language had greatly evolved in recent times. The spoken tongue was even worse.

The Temple historian named Takamoto, who was himself ancient, read the plaque as best he could. The interpreter said, "It says something like 'Don't enter. Injury and death will come to you'."

Brushing his moustache down with a finger, Grey smiled. "That sounds like a curse." Curses were famous in archaeology, starting with the boy-king Tut. The more gullible folk still believed in Tut's curse, which had supposedly killed a number of individuals who'd been part of the expedition that found the tomb in 1922.

Nho added, "It may be more of a warning than a curse. That is more likely."

Undaunted, they continued digging into the night. Midnight came and went. The excitement of a new discovery kept everyone awake, except the monks, who seemed to be taking things in stride. They appeared to be able to sleep standing up, taking catnaps that left them fully awake for another few hours. This was rather remarkable, evidence of the stories of monks' amazing physical feats.

The night passed. Dawn broke over the Pacific Ocean as digging began on the narrow passage to open it up. This did not take long. The main work had been digging around the opening to push stout wooden beams into place to keep the roof from collapsing as the crevice was widened. Four of these had been manhandled down by Grey's laborers, and they were cut to size on the spot. Lintels and columns were placed.

Once the passage was wide enough to admit a man, Nho insisted on entering first. Grey said he had no problem with this. He followed the short Japanese in. The chamber, he found upon spraying light about with his flashlight, was barren and high ceilinged, very high. It was not a hidden repository of either treasure – which was unexpected – or wisdom in the form of ancient scrolls, the more likely outcome. A plain slab lay in the center of the empty cavern, and upon it lay a life-like figure. The flashlight beam revealed black evidence of a fire, but nothing else.

No one spoke as they entered the previously-hidden chamber. Finally, at the slab, Grey said, "I've never heard of anything like this."

Nho said, "I do not understand this." His almond eyes went to Takamoto, who said, "Neither do I. I have never heard of anything like this. There is nothing in our records about it."

The four men – they were joined by the interpreter – crowded around the slab, and studied the figure upon it without touching it. Dressed in a gown that was little more than rags and dust now, it was remarkably well preserved if it was a corpse. It did not look like one. It also did not look *human*. Its skin was a lemony yellow hue, not at all like the more mellow yellow-brown of Asiatics, which ranged from dark to light depending on distance from the equator. And it possessed large lower canines, resembling the tusks of a boar. Its ears were large and scalloped like bat's wings or the fins of certain fish.

"This must be some sort of ceremonial dummy," Grey observed. "Perhaps an effigy embodying some intangible evil?"

Nho said, "I have never heard of such a thing." Glancing at the sect's historian, he asked, "Brother Takamoto?"

That personage said, "Neither have I. I do not know what this is. It appears to be a mannequin of an *oni*."

"*Oni?*" queried the Englishman.

The interpreter explained after listening to Nho, "An *oni* was a demon who was evil and lived to torment humans. They were cannibals ... that is, they consumed human flesh. They were either evil ghosts who refused to go to the afterlife, or men who were so evil they refused to die."

"I cannot imagine what a figure of an *oni* would be doing here," Nho declared.

"There is nothing in our records," affirmed Takamoto, who was visibly disturbed by the entire affair.

After exchanging glances, the four gazed upon the monstrous yellow face of the figure.

Then, the closed eyelids snapped open, revealing red eyes!

Suddenly, the *oni* was off the slab and standing, now of enormous size such that his stooped shoulders scraped the roof of the cavern. He cackled with glee as one scythe-like fingernail skewered the nearest human, raising him high into the air to be pulled off the claw-like nail with his teeth to be consumed whole. The demon chewed on his repast, one human leg hanging out of his mouth like a long, straggling noodle until it was sucked into the bloody maw. He then spit out the bones when he was done, clean and white.

The panicked men attempted to flee. Even widened as it was, the opening was a bottleneck, and no one could pass through because everyone tried to do so at the same time. With two great strides, the *oni* cut off the men's sole escape route.

One by one, he devoured the too-curious visitors, then licked his yellow face clean with a long, forked tongue, and, delicately, scooped up their souls off the cavern floor with his long fingernails as if they were paper dolls. Holding them up before his grotesque face, the demon studied them as if they were insects on pins.

It was dusk by the time the *oni* arrived in Kyoto, once again at human height, three miles from Mount Hiei. His grotesque features showed surprise at the city he had known as Heian-Kyo, called *Yorozuyo no Miya* ("The Eternal City") by Emperor Saga in 810. Emperor Kanmu had moved the capital there from nearby Nagaoka-kyo, which started the Heian Period in Japan. He had started with the palace, which was built at the north end of the main thoroughfare as a sign of power, and then constructed outward. Unlike the previous capital, Buddhist temples were allowed in Heian, in order to bless or protect the city. The palace was still standing. The *oni* recognized it.

The Obon celebration was in full swing when the

demon arrived in Heian. Red and white paper, lucky colors, adorned the city. Obon was a festival of honoring the dead, who were said to return at this time to visit their living relatives. This, combined with the costumes some revelers wore, caused it to be compared to Halloween. But they were quite different. The city offered a carnival with rides, games, and summer festival foods, showing the lighter side of the celebration. But for individuals, it was more somber. On the first day of Obon, which was a three-day affair, families took *chochin* lanterns to graveyards to call the souls of their ancestors back to Earth. On Nakanuhi, the second day, family members spent the day praying to their ancestors at the altar in their home. Today was the final day of Obon, and the festival was wrapping up. Tonight was the Burning of the Character Big on Mount Hiei, which sent ancestors back to the afterlife, signaling the end of Bon *matsuri* – the Obon festival.

The demon from Mount Hiei had no intention of returning whence he'd come.

Absorbing events around him, the *oni* asked a young boy who happened to be standing beside him, "What year is it?"

He was astonished to hear the answer: 2023.

Looking up at the grotesque face of the demon, the boy, taking his features for a mask, asked, "Who are you supposed to be?"

The oni answered, "Kagidzume." This was a compound word of two characters. The first meant "hook" and the second "fingernail". Together, they meant "claw".

Frowning, the boy said, "I've never heard of you".

Kagidzume replied, "You will."

## Chapter 2

## THE RIP VAN WINKLE SYNDROME

August 17, 2023
Yucatan, Mexican Gulf Coast

On a stone slab covered in large broad leaves, a nude bronze-skinned man slept fitfully. He was on the short side and thick-bodied, denoting Native American ancestry. Gray tinged the sideburns of his jet black hair, which fell to his broad shoulders.

Dim dawn light filtered into the large-blocked stone chamber from above, through narrow shafts designed to bring air into the ancient structure as well as illumination. The room possessed a number of niches around it. These were filled with both the ordinary and extraordinary, the former being clothing and cooking implements and the like, while the latter consisted of strange artifacts of Mesoamerican cultures.

The middle-aged fellow awoke with a start. He seemed surprised at his surroundings, until he realized he was awake, and began to calm down. The nightmare had badly rattled him.

Closing his eyes and calming his spirit for a few moments, the fellow proceeded to dress, donning the garb of an ancient people stored in one niche. He then worked his way through the maze of stone-walled passages of the structure, emerging from a ramshackle temple into the verdant green of coastal Central America. The Gulf of Mexico was visible in the distance.

He took deep cleansing breaths, then walked purposefully across a small courtyard to a giant stone head, for which the Olmecs, the first Mesoamerican civilization – they were the first to develop a writing system in the Western hemisphere, in fact – were known for. These often appeared to be wearing headgear, suggesting a player of the Mesoamerican ballgame, a staple of all later cultures such as the Mayans and the Aztecs. No two stone heads were alike, with realistic features suggesting they were representations of actual men. But who the giant stone heads were supposed to be and what their purpose was was not truly known, though theories abounded. One wilder theory posited they were space aliens who gave the Olmecs their knowledge.

Standing before the colossal disembodied stone head, which was nearly ten feet in diameter, the bronze-skinned temple-dweller pulled from a sheath a small obsidian blade, the lower portion wrapped in tanned hide for gripping, and held it up before the statue as if presenting it for inspection. He then carefully applied the razor-sharp tip to his scrotum, and pierced it deeply enough to draw blood.

As scarlet drops fell to the stone courtyard, he then said aloud in a tongue unspoken for centuries, "Great father, I seek your counsel. I have had a dream. A great evil has awakened. It is like nothing I have ever encountered, nor even *sensed* before."

Though its thick stone lips did not move, the colossal head spoke nonetheless. "Is that all, my son?"

"I saw it come here to the Americas from elsewhere ... in the future. I believe this was a premonition dream."

"Cut the head off the snake before it has a chance to strike," counseled the stone head.

"Of course," replied the other. A hint of annoyance underlay his tone. The problem with mysticism was that it was rarely clear, and responses sometimes couched in vague terminology. "Thank you, great father."

The giant stone head did not respond. It was silent once more.

The man returned to his chamber in the abandoned temple, and attended to his wound. According to ancient ritual, soft tissue had to be pierced to summon magic. The tongue was usually used, but other places were equally acceptable.

This thing Dr. Armando Jose Ramirez y Catalan knew before he had found the temple, long ago abandoned and hidden by the jungle which had overgrown it since the passing of the Olmecs some two thousand years earlier. The rest he had learned from the giant stone head.

Ramirez, born in Mexico with Mayan blood on his paternal grandmother's side while his mother was a Catalan beauty, had been about forty in 1922 when he located the temple, after a decade of earning degrees in archaeology, anthropology, and history, followed by a decade of traipsing the globe in search of the peoples and places he'd learned about in various universities. Ramirez knew as much about the Olmecs as anyone, which was to say, almost nothing. Now, a hundred years later, much about them was *still* a mystery.

But not so much to Ramirez.

Armed with a flashlight, his revolver holstered on his hip, he led the men of his expedition through the structure. These consisted of a college teaching assistant and native laborers.

It had taken some time to unearth the covered portion where the entrance lay, but when this was done, exploration of the temple began. Ramirez soon found a stone plate with glyphs on it – what Egyptians would call a "scarab". This was the Mesoamerican version, and worth the price of his entire expedition. The market for pre-Columbian art was booming.

In place, Ramirez rubbed the scarab clean and studied its glyphs. "Protector ... Tamoanchan," he read aloud. "Tamoanchan", the archaeologist knew, came from the Mayans: Meaning "the place of the misty sky", it was the home of their gods. He also knew the Mayans had adopted some of Olmec culture as their own, even using a similar script, just as the later Aztecs had done with the Toltecs. And one of the Mayan's greatest gods, Kukulcan the Feathered Serpent, had come to them from Olmec religion. The Aztecs knew him as Quetzalcoatl.

An Aztec death goddess whose name meant "obsidian butterfly", Itzpapalotl reigned in Tamoanchan, ruling the Tzizimimeh, colloquially known as "demons" who represented the stars that could only be seen during solar eclipses – otherwise, the Sun's light obscured their presence. They were said to be able to come to Earth during such eclipses or during the New Fire ceremony, which the Aztecs held every fifty-two years to usher in a new cycle. All the fires in the city were put out, and a new one was lit on the chest of a captive, and his heart cut out. This single fire was taken throughout the city, re-lighting new fires to ensure the Sun would return for each of the 18980 days of the new calendar cycle.

Ramirez gazed upward, not seeing much due to the little light that penetrated the covering of the temple. No eclipse was due in the region but it *was* a

New Fire calendar year.

Stuffing the scarab into his khaki trousers, the archaeologist led the way to the next chamber. The interior of the temple had fared better than the exterior, and only one section remained beyond the expedition's reach due to a cave-in.

Ramirez insisted on having it dug out. Some days passed while this was done. Finally, when a path was clear, the archaeologist passed through it. On the other side was a mostly intact chamber in which a large mirror stood – larger than the height of a man. Ramirez recognized its metal as copper, one of the minerals known to pre-Columbians. He marveled at it as his laborers entered behind him.

Spying a smudge on the smooth surface of the copper, Ramirez moved to wipe it clean. But it appeared the smudge was *moving*.

The archaeologist looked more closely to determine if, somehow, the mirror itself was moving, creating a strange illusion. But he found that it was not. He cast his gaze about the chamber to look for a source of a shadow that might be causing the phenomenon, but could not locate one. In fact, he shaded the dark area with a hand and then illuminated it with his flashlight, and what he saw greatly disturbed him – the smudge *was* moving!

And, he noted upon closer inspection, it was growing!

As the size of the smudge increased, becoming clearer, it formed an image. Ramirez could discern several moving figures – but these were indistinct. As they grew, he began to make these out. Adorned with skulls around their waists, they could only be called demons.

Ramirez stumbled back, startled. Gasps, murmurs, and exclamations came from his men behind him as they now, too, saw what was occurring. In a matter of seconds, the figures were life sized – and they began emerging from the beaten copper surface of the mirror!

The archaeologist's men, familiar with the dangers of the wild country, began firing their rifles. These had no effect on the invading demons, who resembled animated skeletons. Each wielded a wooden club with razor-sharp obsidian chips set into it, and fell upon the workers.

One came at Ramirez, swung the club. The startled archaeologist fumbled for his pistol. But he was too late. Before he could wrench it free of its holster, a club came down at him.

A bright light erupted as the club's sharp chips struck him – or seemed to. He felt no pain, not even an impact from the blow. He was too enrapt by this that he did not hear the dying cries of his men as they were slaughtered.

Ramirez suddenly noticed a glow emanating from his beltline – where he had wedged the scarab. Feverishly, he pulled it out – it *was* glowing. The demon which had attacked him shrunk back from the golden light.

Emboldened, Ramirez pursued it, until it retreated back into the mirror, disappearing.

The archaeologist called out to the other demons in both Aztec and Mayan, displaying the glowing scarab for all to see. With shrieks of panic, the inhuman creatures retreated back into the mirror, fading from sight.

Examining it with his flashlight, Ramirez saw no blemishes on the copper surface of the mirror.

Then, for the first time, the archaeologist saw the carnage about him. To a man, the workers were dead, their bodies sliced by the obsidian chips that were as sharp as surgical steel scalpels, and causing each to bleed to death in moments. They were covered in blood.

Ramirez retreated, finding one laborer in the corridor outside. He had died fleeing, fatally wounded. Using a stick of dynamite that had been brought to open the closed passage if necessary, he sealed it again. Then he dragged the lone corpse outside, and performed the New Fire ritual that marked the beginning of a new cycle, his face hard set and stony as he cut the heart from his native worker.

Exhausted, Ramirez collapsed and fell asleep. He awakened a century later. When he explored the ruins, the great colossal head explained to him that he was now the protector of Earth, guarding against the return of Itzpapalotl armed with both mystical knowledge and the blazing "scarab".

Ramirez had misinterpreted the glyphs on the scarab: It did not *guard* Tamoanchan, but guarded Earth *against* those residing in Tamoanchan.


Ramirez meditated upon the location of the great evil he had sensed – somewhere other than the Americas. He *felt* it – and then, abruptly, it was gone, before he could pinpoint its foreign locale. He'd been too late.

Donning a ceremonial jade mask, Ramirez made to leave the temple. Speaking a few words of the Olmec tongue, time and space bent as the *Blazing Scarab* traveled to New York City.

## Chapter 3

## GUILD HOUSE

August 17, 2023
New York City

From the air, Guild House resembled a fortress, a large structure with a small, enclosed courtyard. In reality, it was a collection of townhouses that had been bought one by one and transformed into a single building that occupied an entire city block on the upper East Side of Manhattan near Central Park. One townhouse that was larger than the others dominated the complex, sitting in the middle of the block. Behind it, two smaller residences lay. These were bounded on either side by homes that were half the size of the largest one, closing in the back lawn, making it a courtyard of sorts.

The Blazing Scarab appeared, stepping out of interdimensional space into reality. Alone in the main conference room of Guild House, he moved to a control panel, and pressed a large red button.

Alarms began to whoop. The Blazing Scarab did not move, and abruptly, the door to the spacious chamber opened, admitting a small, lanky dark-haired man in a dark suit. His pinched face was tight with tension.

"Blazing Scarab," he breathed in a combination of relief and annoyance when he saw the figure in the room.

The uberhero nodded. "*Hola*, Thompson."

"You really should check in when you come in, you know," Thompson said sourly. "That *is* procedure."

"I am well aware of your government procedures," replied the Blazing Scarab. "But this *is* an emergency ... as I am sure your security system informed you." He gestured upward to the shrieking alarm. "You might dispense with that."

Pulling a walkie-talkie from beneath his jacket, Thompson did just that.

Then the two men waited.


In a modern glass-and-steel tower that overlooked the Hudson River, a middle-aged man in a wheelchair watched a computer monitor, its bright image reflecting off his horn-rimmed glasses. He looked twenty years older than he was, his body debilitated by disease.

Seeing the special alarm signal that signified need of his presence, he rolled himself into a private chamber of the main room of his laboratory and, going to the desk, placed a metal band upon his brow; wires connected it to machine, one of many in the chamber. The crippled scientist then typed CEREBEX to bring up the program. This was a hidden program that could only be located by a specific search for it by name.

A few blocks away, in a warehouse, a light came on, revealing a large green metallic man who stood stock still in a charging dock. He stood eight feet tall, with bulky torso and large, smooth limbs, resembling to some degree the robot of the 1939 New York City World's Fair, Elektro, built by Westinghouse. He went into motion, leaving the dock. Going to a particular spot in the empty warehouse, Cerebex dropped into the water below, and made his way to the shore some distance from the warehouse, where he climbed onto land, and, firing rockets from his feet, launched himself into the air in the direction of Guild House.


Bluish light arced over the surface of what resembled a shepherd's crook, held by a small man in magenta-hued armor who floated in the air in an alley above a man clothed in a radiation suit. The emblem of three interlocking ellipses signifying atomic power adorned the torso of the latter. His ungloved hands glowed golden.

"Surrender, Dr. Fission," said the armored man; rather than covering him fully as traditional armor of the Middle Ages did, his armor was composed of large plates over an under suit of modern chain mail. "You are a scientist. You know your radiation cannot penetrate my magnetic bubble."

"I'll never surrender, Magno," spat Dr. Fission, his hands glowing even more brightly.

The alarm in Magno's metal suit sounded. Using his staff, the young uberhero – his helmet exposed a "T" shape of flesh similar to the helmets of the ancient Greeks, revealing him as young, Asian, and male; its visor was large and boomerang shaped – quickly brought a drainpipe down onto Dr. Fission's head, knocking him out. The pipe then wrapped itself around the criminal, binding him tightly.

"My apologies, Doctor," the magnetic uberhero told his captive foe. "I must attend to an emergency."

As he sped away to join his colleagues in the Guild, Magno alerted the police to his enemy's location via radio built into his suit before the ubervillain could awaken and melt his way free of his impromptu bonds.

Dr. Nemesis, wearing a diving suit of his own design, with an oversized clear rectangular bubble helmet that permitted vision in every direction, floated over mysterious ruins on the ocean floor off Antarctica. He received the emergency signal, and ignored it.

Dr. Evelyn Martin idly glanced down at the name in her appointment book. Amirah Hussin. Late again. The therapist displayed none of the small habits others did when annoyed, such as tapping fingers on the desk.

The bell rang, signaling the arrival of someone. Dr. Martin went to the door, opened it to find her patient there.

"Sorry I'm late," said Amirah, her brown eyes carrying the impression of sincerity. She was short, slim, with dusky skin, her hair covered by *hijab*, which left the face exposed, unlike the *niqaq*. Dr. Martin knew that her patient was a thoroughly Americanized Muslim, having been born in the country after her parents fled the Middle East in the Eighties.

"It's your money, Poppy," Dr. Martin, a fiftyish blonde with a build that was turning matronly. "However, there are others who could use my help if you don't want to be here."

"I do," said Poppy Hussin. "You know I work at night and sometimes it's hard for me to get here on time in the morning."

"If I recall correctly," countered Dr. Martin, "you are just as tardy in the afternoon."

"I know," admitted Poppy.

"Kleptomania isn't a big problem ... like, say alcoholism. It doesn't hurt anyone. If it's not that important to you to solve, you don't have to see me, you know."

"I know, but it *is* important to me," Poppy explained.

Then the young Muslim's phone rang. Sort of. It sounded more like an alarm than a ring tone, a low *whoop-whoop-whoop*.

Poppy looked at it, muttering, "Sorry. This is an emergency."

After a moment, she added, "This really is an emergency, Doctor. I've *got* to go. Sorry!"

"I've got to bill you for the hour," Dr. Martin called after her patient.

"I know," Poppy returned over her shoulder.


Tall and "film star handsome" with coal-dark hair, Monroe Staley, Jr. stood before his senior staff, which was gathered around an oblong table on the upper floor of the administration building of the company his father had founded. "You mean to tell me the Air Guard system still isn't working?"

The men at the table nodded solemnly. One finally said, "We could submit it to the Department of Defense now, and retool it with additional funding."

"My *name* is on this company, and *Staley* doesn't play that game," spat the eponymous head of Staley Aircraft Technologies International. "We're either going to scrap it or put more money into it ourselves.

"I want recommendations on my desk by the end of business. And if this *ever* happens again – "

## 22

The tabletop buzzed. The source was a computer screen built into the rich dark wood.

Glancing at the message there, Staley growled, "Get out. All of you. *Now.*"

His senior staff hurried to obey, scurrying away like rats. It seemed that whatever the call was, it had quite possibly saved at least one man's job.

Once the chamber was empty, Staley went to a wall, opened a secret panel, and stepped into an elevator. This descended to a hidden subterranean world that had belonged to the original Staley Aircraft Company built by Monroe's father. This had either been refurbished or built over as the company was modernized with the advent of transistors in the Sixties, when his father had still been relatively young, and refurbished again when the son took over the company. Monroe Staley, Sr. had died an old man, leaving behind a beautiful ex-starlet wife and infant son. There was a lot of speculation about the elder Staley during his lifetime, but that's all anyone really knew of his death. He'd been hurriedly buried without an autopsy.

Monroe Staley stepped out of the elevator when it reached its destination, and, going to a small niche, began drawing on the red, white, and blue armored "Fighting Yank" suit.

A bright costume flashed across the Brooklyn rooftops as the figure in it leaped and ran single-mindedly. Dynamic Man's red hair fluttered in the breeze above his yellow mask. His costume was mostly yellow, trimmed in red, which included a large red breastplate that was bulletproof. Yellow discs hung on his crimson belt.

Brooklyn College was just in sight when the belt

buckle of Dynamic Man's costume buzzed. The young redheaded uberhero turned and glanced toward Manhattan, then back again at his destination.

Turning back toward the island, he started off in that direction, muttering, "Shit."


Roddy Corcoran, medium-sized and lanky in his three-piece suit with a carnation in its lapel and grasping a cane that he did not need, watched in silence as Gregorio, one of the city's hottest photographers, took shots of Ling Lu Pei – commonly called "Pei Pei", her working name. She was not only trim, but athletic, the fashion reporter noted as she moved gracefully from pose to pose. Her hair was short, cut pageboy style – her trademark; she resisted attempts to have it styled any other way, refused to grow it long although a cosmetic firm had offered her a small fortune to let it grow long. Pei Pei already had a small fortune, and was more concerned about her brand than acquiring another fortune. Roddy himself had covered the story, so he knew about the brouhaha in the fashion world firsthand.

He waited patiently to interview the beautiful Asian model, admiring her not with the look of a male for a female, but as someone who took pleasure in viewing a work of fine art.

After the session was over, Pei Pei came to Roddy, whom she knew of despite never having met him before.

"How did you like it, Mr. Corcoran?" she asked as she neared him.

"You're everything I imagined you'd be, having seen your photos. And call me 'Roddy'."

"I will take that as a compliment, Roddy," Pei Pei smiled.

"You should," the angular fashion reporter returned with a smile.

At that moment, two signals sounded. As each checked their phones, Pei Pei said, "Excuse me, I have to take this."

Roddy gestured with his phone, "My editor."

A few seconds later, the two agreed to reschedule their interview.

Not many minutes later in the alley outside the building where the photo shoot had just finished, the Flame, garbed in a red costume with flame-like yellow trim, spun at the soft sound behind him. He spun, a hand extended in self-defense, to find a woman there. She wore a textured ebony cat suit that only exposed her eyes, which were black and almond-shaped, and her very long black hair.

"You surprised me, Black Fury," said the Flame.

"Sorry," returned the uberheroine. "When I saw you, I thought we might travel to the Guild House together ... since you are in the area."

"What a coincidence," admitted the Flame in a pointed tone. "Shall we?"

Black Fury gestured to a small speedy-looking coupe behind her that was one-of-a-kind.


Nurse Higgins mopped the sweat off the brow of Dr. Emmett Tillman as he was finishing surgery on a patient. When his watch buzzed, the twenty-something surgeon said, "Dr. Fenrick, will you take over here and close up?"

"Of course, Emmett," said Fenrick, who had very black hair and a big nose that was set off by a bushy moustache. "Is everything all right?"

"An urgent case I need to look into," returned Dr. Tillman as he backed away from the table, stripped off his surgical gloves, and departed the operating theater. On the walk to his office, he checked his phone for the full message, and when he got there, he used the hospital line to call the operator. "This is Dr. Tillman. I need the assistance of one of our interns, M'Bele Obatu. It's urgent."

Moments later, the surgeon heard the page come over the hospital's PA system, and, after a few minutes, a young black man entered the office.

"The Crusader and Jinx are needed," Emmett Tillman announced.


When the last of the Guild members arrived at their headquarters, they found a solemn-faced Blazing Scarab. It was clear that *he* had sent the emergency alert. By the looks on the others' faces, he had not yet explained *why* he had sent the summons. He did so now.

"I know not all of you are on active duty with the Guild at this time," said the Hispanic uberhero. "But I have sensed a very great threat that will require all our power and skill to find and defeat."

He then told his teammates of the dream he'd had.

## Chapter 4

## THE WITCHING HOUR

October 31, 2024
New York City

The night-black thing flew through the dark skies over Manhattan noiselessly. It arced high then began to descend rapidly, and it soon became clear the man-sized object was not flying at all, but falling. It had been launched, and scribed a parabolic arc as it traveled at an inhuman speed. It struck a skyscraper at midnight, the witching hour, not far from its origin point, with all the force of a small meteorite and the noise of a bomb exploding – though no light or heat accompanied the devastation.

The upper portion of the tower of the skyscraper exploded under the tremendous impact, throwing debris into the cool night air. The top of the building, which was empty, housing mechanicals, comprised the largest of these chunks. This slowly toppled off the structure, plummeting down to land on several automobiles below stopped in traffic, crushing their occupants. The accompanying debris blocked all lanes of traffic.

Smaller bits of stone and glass and steel fell to the street, largely missing those below because the earlier drop had brought traffic to a standstill. Both drivers who had evacuated their vehicles and pedestrians were now straining to look up to find the cause of the falling detritus, so no one was injured this time. This smaller debris was as deadly as the fallen tower but added little to the destruction on the street. The larger section of the skyscraper had flattened everything there was to flatten. It now seemed relatively safe, everything loose above apparently having already fallen to the ground. The concern now was for those who resided in the upper levels of the building. The worst of it looked to be over.

No one could guess the carnage had just begun.

Firemen and policemen alike rushed to the scene, unaware that an attack had taken place. The assumption was a small meteorite had struck, and initial eyewitness accounts seemed to confirm this – those who happened to be looking skyward at the time. People on the street who only knew of the tower falling and in the lower sections of the skyscraper who had come outside to see what had occurred, awakened by the falling tower if not the initial impact, knew nothing helpful.

But soon, new information came in. These latter witnesses explained that the entire building had shaken, suggesting a cause for the collapse of the tower: Something powerful had occurred, either an explosion or an impact. Rumors of another 9-11-type attack began to circulate – though there had been no explosion, no fire. Perhaps this time, the detonation had failed.

The unknown missile that had struck the building had not exited. Whatever it was, it was still lodged within. Rescue workers and police officers began to ascend the skyscraper to learn the truth.

As they did so, something emerged from the

skyscraper's gaping wound, perching itself on a jagged ledge. Between the distance to the ground and its night-black hue, it was all but invisible to those far below. But residents in nearby skyscrapers who had been awakened by the thunderous collision got glimpses of it as it moved in the dim moonlight. It was larger than a man and covered in black metal, in fact big enough to be a man *wearing* armor that was intricate and stylized. The human face, if there was one, was fully concealed beneath a helmet.

Moving toward a damaged wall, the armored figure pressed itself against it and pushed. The wall fell to the street below, creating a new panic – despite onlookers having been shooed away from the block by a police cordon by this time. But there were still plenty of building residents who were being evacuated to be concerned about further debris falling.

Binoculars were located and put into use. The cop in charge below exclaimed, "There's a robot up there!"

This declaration was punctuated by another section of debris falling nearby, landing with the report of a thunderbolt.

The police changed their strategy of evacuation. The officer in charge waited for an opening then gave the all clear sign, and in small groups, the residents were taken to safety between the impacts of falling debris.

With the elevators to the upper floor having been destroyed by the initial collision of the "robot" with the building, city workers had a long climb after reaching the limit of the lower elevators. They were still on their way up when a police chopper arrived to stop the robot on a rampage.

It first ignored the calls from the bullhorn to cease and desist, then the bullets of the high-powered rifles.

These ricocheted off the black armor without leaving so much as a scratch. The officers inside the helicopter wished they had a bazooka but this was not standard ordnance for the chopper team.

Their presence had proved useless.

After reporting the results, the helicopter was ordered back to base. Others had been called in to take up the fight.

The policemen who had ascended the tower to aid rescue workers in evacuating upper floor residents were duly informed, and ordered not to engage the robot: They were to guard the rescuers and any survivors, and only act if the armored figure attempted to attack *people*, leaving it alone to destroy what was left of the upper section of the building.

While the rescue workers started with those trapped on the lower floors, a pair of officers scouted ahead. Wind whistled above them as they climbed the last of the stairs – the night sky above was open to them where the skyscraper simply ended.

They were surrounded by devastation. Anyone who had lived at this height must surely be dead, they realized. It would have been impossible to have survived the initial impact.

Noise caught the attention of the pair of cops. Knowing what was causing it, they gazed about until their eyes fell upon the black robot. It was leveling the exposed upper floor, clearing it off as if tidying up a home before visitors arrived, seemingly oblivious to the presence of the two men.

The cops watched in fascination and horror when, finishing its job, the robot disappeared down a hole and began dismantling the next layer of the building. Though they lost sight of it, they could hear its actions. It sounded like demolition performed by a bulldozer – minus the sound of a diesel motor.

The stairwell wall suddenly collapsed – and there stood the giant black robot!

Then he continued his rampage, ignoring the two cops. Neither man moved, for fear of catching the robot's attention.

Then, when its back was turned toward them, they quickly retreated down the stairs.


In short order, three other suits of armor crashed to the earth on the island of Manhattan in the seconds after midnight with similar violence and destruction. The sites ringed Central Park in a crude diamond shape, not that anyone noticed this fact so early in the attack.

In a skyscraper not far away, thin yellow lips on a grotesque face covered in parchment-like skin parted, and murmured, "*Soshite sore ga hajimarimasu* ...."

The handful of Japanese men dressed in the company of the Claw, in their black suits and colorful shirts with white collars and wingtip shoes, understood, despite their language having evolved since their master's time – "And so it begins ...."

The thin yellow lips curled back to produce a smile exposing sharp, fang-like teeth in expectation of widespread death and destruction this night.

## Chapter 5

## THE NAME IS DEATH

By the time the police had responded to the rampages of the four armored figures around the island, Guild House had been notified. At this time of night, a skeleton crew worked the headquarters, since no members were in permanent residence, and all but one team member was absent from the headquarters. The member on duty this night, Kitten, was not asleep when the alert came in. Though she was short and thin and her breasts small, her hips flared enough to signify she was an adult if diminutive woman. She possessed a lithe athletic figure, which was sheathed in a skin-tight suit of dark blue that seemed to fluctuate in actual shade. It actually lightened in hue when direct light was shone on it, and near-black in dim light, making the young uberheroine almost invisible. The costume possessed a bob tail and perky cat's ears. Short whiskers on the cheeks detected chemicals in the air, more accurate than any human sense of smell. Claws curled over the fingers and toes, so that when these were bent, the claws stuck out for climbing – or fighting. A dew claw was always exposed on each of the heels.

Stretching like her namesake, seemingly *growing* several inches in the process, Kitten padded to Thompson's office in the Security section, which was housed in an adjoining structure from the "main house". The alert had come in there, since the G-man was the team's national security liaison, ostensibly working for the Secret Service. Not being a member of the team, the lanky agent worked as an advisor, so it was Kitten who sent out the emergency summons to all current members, active and reserve, upon learning of the content of the alert. One by one, the members filtered into Guild House over the next half hour.

Garbed in severe black clothing that was reminiscent of pilgrim attire, Dr. Death was a shadow in the blackness of the near-moonless night. Once, his face had been painted like a skull. Now his visage was truly deathly – gaunt, pale, *unhealthy* looking. His physical deterioration showed in his movements as well. He did not move swiftly among the rooftops.

The Crusader and Jinx had no trouble keeping up with the ubervillain. In fact, the pair could have easily caught him. But in fact they paced him, never letting Dr. Death get more than a glimpse of them, the Crusader in his white and blue costume – the colors of the United Nations – and Jinx in red, black, and green – the colors of the pan-African movement. The older uberhero's collar and mask, belt, boots, and gloves were blue, the remainder white. The protégé's tunic was red; domino mask, sleeves, and leggings black, as was a short cape that could be drawn about his torso to hide the bright hue of his tunic, making the youth almost invisible in the dark; and boots, gloves, and trunks green.

"I cannot believe he has not suspected we are following him to his lair," murmured Jinx, padding alongside the Crusader.

"He thinks he's smarter than we are," his mentor

replied.

"Is he not smarter than we are?"

"People believe what they want to believe. He wants to believe he's smarter than us, so he thinks we're easy to outwit. I submit we're not," answered the Crusader. "And even if he gets away, we stopped his latest mass murder scheme. That's the important thing – saving lives."

Dr. Death was known to live up to his codename. He was a homicidal manic who blamed society for somewhat vague reasons, something about too many rotten apples had spoiled the barrel, and the mad scientist felt the need for a reset of humanity. Those that survived would be better than previous generations. Societal Darwinism. Dr. Death had pointed to the absolute idiocy of American citizens, displayed every day on the internet – not to mention endless wars and climate change.

After several blocks, the black-swathed murderer descended to the street near the waterfront via a fire escape. The pair of uberheroes trailed him to a decrepit warehouse. After giving him a minute, the Crusader followed him inside.

A shiny blade rapidly descended toward the humanitarian hero. Only his reflexes honed over more than a decade of action saved him from death – he stopped short, and the oversized axe narrowly missed the uberhero, thunking down hard into the soft wood of the floor.

The Crusader yanked the two halves of his battle staff from his belt, joining them together as he danced away. Spinning, both hands on one end of his battle staff, the Crusader swung it like a bat at the personage who wielded the axe. It collided with a giant in black who was not Dr. Death, causing him to do little more than hesitate in his brutal attack.

"Black Axeman!" exclaimed the Crusader. The ubervillain was garbed in the medieval uniform of a headsman, all black. A matching hood concealed his features. "Since when do you work for Dr. Death?"

From across the room, the sinister ubervillain rasped, "Since I've become too enfeebled to fight my own fights …."

He had the Crusader to thank for that – the enemy who kept hounding him. Dr. Death was not aware that he had been the original's teen sidekick all those years ago when they'd first met, and not the uberhero who'd foiled his first scheme of revenge.

"I've got the Axeman, Jinx," the Crusader said over his shoulder.

"I will take Dr. Death," the young uberhero finished the thought.

The Crusader took up a position between the Black Axeman and his weapon, still standing stuck in the floor. The killer criminal towered over the Crusader and outweighed him by a good fifty pounds. When the staff came at him again, he threw back his arms and stuck out his chest. He seemed not to feel the impact when it came a moment later, only letting out a guttural growl in response. He was not known by those who'd faced him to speak in any intelligible manner.

As the Black Axeman marched toward him, the Crusader quickly dismantled his staff into two pieces, and readied himself for the coming attack. He ducked beneath the ubervillain's questing hands, and struck at his knees with the twins clubs.

The giant headsman slapped down at the Crusader with an open hand, catching him by surprise. The uberhero fell back, scrambled to his feet while the Black Axeman wrenched his trapped weapon from the floor with a single yank on the long handle.

A strangled cry from behind the uberhero caught his attention. A quick, desperate glance revealed Jinx in Dr. Death's grasp, his life being leeched away by the toxicity of the ubervillain's touch.

Then everything went black.

When he awoke, the Crusader found himself hanging from the rafters, his hands bound by manacles. Beside him, Jinx hung semi-conscious, while not far below the pair's feet lay a pool of ugly-looking liquid.

"Acid," rasped Dr. Death for explanation.

The uberhero barely had time to take in the situation, still groggy from the Black Axeman's blow that had knocked him out, when he abruptly dropped an inch toward the acid bath below him.

"A ratchet," Dr. Death explained with a death's-head smile. "You and your young partner will drop an inch every minute until the acid slowly consumes you both. *Very* slowly." He cackled madly, which turned into a cough.

"Isn't this a little theatrical, even for you?" queried the Crusader as his eyes darted up to the mechanism above his head. It was far out of his reach, being fastened to the rafters.

"I used to be in the *theater*," Dr. Death smiled.

"Do tell."

"I'm afraid you don't have time to hear my life story, Crusader. I do not have much time left in this life, but it is longer than *you* have." Dr. Death laughed a laugh that sounded like a carpenter dragging a rasp across a piece of wood.

As he watched the two ubervillains depart, the Crusader heard Jinx, beside him, regain consciousness with a moan. His first coherent words upon absorbing the situation were, "This does not look good."

"No, it doesn't," agreed the veteran hero. "I'm sorry I got you into this …."

"No – you gave me a new life after mine was taken from me," Jinx replied. "I am proud to have served with you."

Chapter 6

## THE GREAT ESCAPE

"What's the Obatu boy's story?" asked Emmett Tillman, doctor in charge of the charity hospital that had been set up in central Africa where another civil war was underway. It was one of many over recent decades. Looking at his clipboard, he said, "I don't see any other family members here, or even *listed* ...."

"There's a sister," answered Cliff Darrow, a junior doctor, new to the Doctors Without Borders program. "Parents were murdered."

"The boy soldiers?" Tillman queried.

Darrow, who was young and hawk-faced with sandy hair, nodded. Central Africa was home to armies comprised of teenaged boys and younger. Being immature and inexperienced, they were easier to recruit and control than adults, and more likely to fight for *idealistic* reasons, whether these were valid or not. Five nations in Africa used boy soldiers, and another four in Asia did, as well.

"God-dammit," Tillman muttered under his breath.

"I'm with you," Darrow said in all seriousness. "This place is insane."

The conversation was interrupted by the roar of an aged, muffler-less Jeep.

Going to a window – this was a square cut in the canvas of the big tent with a mosquito net covering the opening – the two doctors watched as the vehicle came to a stop, and its passengers – boy soldiers – hopped out.

"Fuck!" exclaimed Dr. Darrow.

"It'll be all right," Tillman assured the junior doctor in an unusually calm tone. Visits from soldiers were not uncommon, unfortunately, and their feelings usually ambivalent about the safety of those in the hospital camps. As long as the medical staff did as they were told and didn't interfere with whatever the soldiers wanted, they, at least, were unharmed. The same could not be said of all the patients. "Just don't do anything to antagonize them, no matter *what* they do – they could easily kill everyone here. I'll handle this."

"Right, Dr. Tillman," Darrow said in a tight voice. This was his first dealing with a boy army.

"Pass it along – quickly!" the veteran doctor urged without taking his eyes off the approaching soldiers.

Darrow had just conveyed the news when the half-dozen underage soldiers, each carrying a light automatic rifle, entered the tent, which was based on the M.A.S.H. units of the Korean War, except there were no military personnel here, only civilians. Everyone froze in place. Except Emmett Tillman. He met the small force at the doorway.

"Can I help you?" he asked innocently. "Do you have wounded who need medical attention? We don't turn away anyone who needs aid."

"We are looking for soldiers," said the boy in charge. He could not have been older than seventeen years of age.

"There are none here," Tillman explained. "All our patients and all our staff are civilians."

The teenaged soldier grinned broadly, revealing a silvery metal front tooth. Gold was too valuable here for dental work. "I know. We will take boys to join our army." He raised his rifle up to his side, holding it prominently as he pointed its barrel upward.

"No one here is ready to be released," Tillman explained in an even tone, "or else they would have been. Everyone here is still being treated."

"That does not matter to me," said the teenager. "I will decide who can come with us."

"Have you a medical degree?" Tillman asked lightly. But he was not smiling.

The boy soldier swung the butt of his rifle up at the American. Tillman's hand whipped out, caught the rifle.

As the teen struggled to free his weapon from the grip of Tillman, the doctor said, "It's not smart to pick on a stranger. You might get a nasty surprise." He let the boy unsuccessfully try to wrest the rifle from his grasp. Several moments passed without any change to the status quo. When the young officer opened his mouth to bark an order to his followers, the doctor threw his body into the boy, knocking him back into his soldiers. Three toppled. Two staggered back, one managing to stay upright.

Tillman vaulted over those on the ground, twisting sideways mid-air. His horizontal body caught both boys, knocking them down. All three ended up on the ground. The American swiftly, decisively, put the pair out of the fight with two quick blows.

Spinning, he found the other three struggling to their feet.

Leaping, he spread his arms, caught all three. One slipped aside. Tillman kicked him in the gut while he struck one then another of the boy soldiers – the latter the commander of the unit. He then finished off the final teen.

Tillman was getting to his feet when Darrow

rushed up beside him. The young doctor exclaimed, "I've never seen anything like that!"

Ignoring the declaration, Tillman told his subordinate, "Start evacuation procedures! We're moving farther away from the fighting!"

As his staff quickly moved to obey, Tillman injected each of the boy soldiers with a sedative that would keep them unconscious until long after the hospital had departed, removed the ammo from each of their weapons, throwing it out into the brush, and took the distributor cap off the Jeep's motor, stranding the boys. He then joined his staff in their work.

Fourteen months later, M'Bele Obatu came to the United States with his older sister N'Longa, whom Emmett Tillman had married to speed the immigration process. The two teenagers, grateful though deeply puzzled by the aid, queried their benefactor, who explained simply, "I'm paying it forward. Someone once did something like this for me and I'm repaying his kindness."


The Crusader, glancing about the room, noted, "Dr. Death took away my battle staff" – it lay on the floor well out of reach – "but – "

"He did not expect *me* to carry anything useful," Jinx smiled. "One of my explosives ...."

"No, better use acid," amended the older hero. "We'll need time to get out of the way of the acid bath. An explosive will break the chain instantly and we'll fall into it."

"Right ... of course," murmured Jinx, who was still learning the tradecraft of being an uberhero.

"Get up on my shoulders," the Crusader directed his young partner.

Jinx began swinging his legs – which were not

bound – until he built up enough momentum to close them about the Crusader's neck. He then worked his way up, until he sat on the shoulders of his mentor. The Crusader gritted his teeth under the strain of the extra weight pulling on his wrists. The skin would have been rubbed off if not for his blue gloves.

With his arms relatively free now, Jinx reached into a pouch on his belt and removed a small globe of glass the size of a marble, filled with a liquid. Carefully moving it to one of the links that bound his partner, the young uberhero smashed it against the metal. The acid spilled, and Jinx twisted to protect the Crusader from the excess that dripped down.

He'd applied it to the narrow gap in a link, where the acid would have to do the least amount of work to create an opening. There wasn't enough of the substance to eat through an entire thick link, not in one glass sphere anyway. The weight of the two men on the weakening link did the rest.

The ratchet ticked like a clock, lowering the two men to a horrible death by inches.

As the metal bent and the ends of the link began to stretch apart, Jinx announced, "It is close ...."

"Okay, good work," said the Crusader. "Climb off me so I can swing free when it breaks. I don't want to drop into the acid bath."

Instead of jumping off his mentor's shoulders, Jinx shimmied up the chain to the rafters, where he perched himself as the Crusader began to swing his legs back and forth. When the link finally broke, the uberhero went flying off to one side of the pool, missing it and landing heavily on the floor.

Above, Jinx applied another globe of acid to his own chains, and worked himself free. By this time, the Crusader had located the switch that slid a panel back over the pool of acid, hiding the trap once more.

Then the pair set about getting the manacles off. The Crusader was by no means a gadgeteer, but over the years he had put together a crime-fighting tool kit, based on what police and private detectives used. Being a teenager when he'd first started out as a costumed uberhero as an apprentice to the original Crusader, he lacked the physical prowess and wisdom acquired by experience so made up for it by preparedness. He'd acquired any equipment he could lay in his hands, often confiscating them from criminals, until he had assembled quite a collection. Among these was a lock pick set, with which he opened the manacles.

When this was accomplished, the Crusader retrieved his battle staff, and announced, "Now let's go find Dr. Death and the Black Axeman!"

## Chapter 7

## ENGINE OF DESTRUCTION

The Crusader and Jinx's pursuit of Dr. Death and the Black Axeman was interrupted by a thunderous crash to the north. It sounded like an explosion, but there followed no flash of light, no flames, no heat. But a shockwave rippled through the neighborhood that nearly knocked the two uberheroes off their feet as well as a number of smaller structures off their foundations. Each stumbled but neither fell, regaining their balance quickly.

"That sounds like the call of duty," the Crusader told his young partner in a grim tone.

"Then let us see about it," returned Jinx.

The pair started off in the direction whence the shockwave had emanated. They traveled through several blocks of devastation. The worsening condition of the area as they proceeded told them they were on the right path to find the source of the thunderous noise. Finally, they came upon a tall, black figure in armor. He stood nearly seven feet tall. He was clawing his way out of a small crater in the street.

"What is it?" queried Jinx.

"It appears to be a Japanese samurai," said the Crusader. "Sans *katana*." A "katana" was the sword of a samurai, long and curved and as sharp as a scalpel, the finest blades in the world. "I don't recall seeing black armor before, but there's Japanese flair to that armor."

"How do you know this?"

"I fought the Shinto Samurai when I was the original Crusader's partner," explained the uberhero. "Several times. I learned whatever I could about the samurai. It pays to know your enemy."

Glancing at his young partner, the Crusader said, "Keep an eye on him while I see about the injured." A debris field surrounded the small crater created by the impact of the falling armored individual. Much damage and many injuries had been caused.

The samurai had seemingly fallen from the sky. No plane droned overhead to have dropped him. It was very strange – particularly the fact that the man in the armor appeared uninjured by his long fall.

Jinx watched in silence as the ebony samurai climbed up and reached the street – police had not yet arrived on the scene. But before the Crusader had gotten far in his mission, the samurai went to the nearest automobile. Hefting it easily above his head, he threw it many yards down the block, where it landed on two other vehicles, crumpling them.

Seeing this, the Crusader changed his course – no one was safe if the armored giant was on a rampage. He removed the two pieces of his battle staff from their place on a thigh, and joined them together as he ran toward the invader – for that is what it was, he now knew.

The wail of sirens began to fill the air as emergency responders hurried to the scene. Jinx hurried to intercept them as the red flashing lights came into view. His red, green, and black costume illuminated by headlights brought the speeding vehicles to a stop. He went to the first cop who was getting out of his cruiser as NYC Fire and Rescue began assessing the situation.

Jinx said: "There is an armored giant here. He climbed from a crater, apparently haven fallen from the sky. The Crusader is engaging him now." The young uberhero pointed in the direction of the fight.

The officer shouted his subordinates, "Careful with your bullets! The Crusader is out there!"

As cops fanned out to survey the scene – it looked like Berlin at the end of the second world war here, with piles of rubble along the street – they escorted rescue workers to those trapped in automobiles or lay fallen on the street. They found the crater Jinx had mentioned – the falling samurai had narrowly missed a building. This had been visibly damaged by the shock wave of the impact, but was still standing. For now.

Hearing the noise of metal against stone and metal, one pair of cops followed it until they came upon the samurai and the Crusader. The uberhero held his staff like a bat, the samurai swatting it aside easily as he sought to strike the human. The staff did little more than distract the attention of the ebony soldier from his prey.

As the strange armored figure closed in on the Crusader, the uberhero spun, and used his staff to vault away. The samurai followed, leaping across the gap in the damaged ground.

Seeing their opportunity, some of the rescuers quickly moved into the vacated zone to aid those who had been injured.

Out of one end of the battle staff slid a long blade. The Crusader aimed this for a joint on the samurai armor and jammed the knife in. The armored giant hesitated for a mere moment, then resumed his movement – snapping the blade off as if it were a cheap plastic toy.

Seeing this, the Crusader swung the staff around, pointing it upward. A retractable line shot out of the other end, grappled a jutting piece of building above, and quickly took its owner up out of reach of the samurai's questing metal hands.

After a moment, the engine of destruction turned, and returned to its crusade of terror, apparently having forgotten about the uberhero.


Seeing the failure of his mentor to stop the samurai, Jinx took a slingshot from a small case on his belt, and loaded it with an explosive pellet from another compartment. He carried a variety of these, including smoke, incendiary, acid, explosive, and hard ceramic. He had in fact taken his codename from these weapons, since they caused bad luck to befall his enemies.

Jinx fired. His pellet struck a shoulder and exploded upon impact.

This got the attention of the ebony samurai. Its head slowly moved from side to side seeking its attacker. It saw men in uniforms, and it began moving toward them menacingly.

Jinx responded by shooting a trio of smoke pellets. These broke at the armored giant's feet and spurted obscuring black smoke like juice being squeezed from a lemon. The cool night breeze spread the plumes into a cloud around the samurai.

Grabbing the bullhorn from the startled officer who held it, the young uberhero called out to the unaware workers, "Fall back! The samurai is coming your way!"

The group of men hesitated for a moment, then,

seeing Jinx beside the officer in command holding the bullhorn, hastily retreated to safety.

Stepping out of the smoke, the black samurai peered about for several moments, and, not finding any live prey, returned to his work of demolishing the city of New York like a one-man wrecking crew.

"He don't seem human," vouchsafed the police officer in charge of the scene.

"Perhaps he is not," returned Jinx in a thoughtful tone.

"What does he want?"

"It seems all he wants at the moment is to destroy."

"I doubt our bullets can hurt him any more than your bomb did," said the cop. "We're gonna need bigger back-up. I'm calling SWAT."

He was doing just that when he noticed Jinx moving toward the ebony engine of destruction. "Hey, where are you going, kid?"

Without any resentment in his tone at being called "kid" – Jinx was nineteen years old – the young uberhero said over his shoulder, "To join my partner."

He then directed his attention on the path ahead, and fell into silence as he weaved his way through scattered debris, ducking to stay out of sight.


Taking advantage of his young partner's smoke diversion, the Crusader put some distance between himself and the black samurai, and when the armored giant resumed his destructive rampage, the uberhero, perched up on a wall that was still standing, began lobbing bits of concrete and stone at it to keep it away from rescue workers who were tending to the injured, and police officers who were moving to surround the thing. The ebon giant reacted in the simplest method possible: He charged into the wall, bringing it and the Crusader down.

Being a veteran crime-fighter, the uberhero knew how to fall and how to land. He avoided serious injury, and was in motion again a moment after hitting the ground. He leaped up away from the samurai's arms.

As it sought out its enemy, the samurai ignored small explosions around it sent by Jinx – his mentor being too close for a direct attack upon the samurai to be safe, so his attack was diversionary in nature. When the young uberhero could see the Crusader scramble away, out of reach of the ebony-armored figure, he shot explosives straight at it. It hefted a small automobile in what appeared to be an annoyed manner, and flung it at the source of its seeming pique, Jinx.

The young man flung himself to the ground as the vehicle went wildly over his head, crashing into a nearby building. Debris came down as a result, a cloud of dust enveloping Jinx. Amid it, as he hurried to his feet, he stepped sideways on a chunk of concrete and twisted his ankle, and crashed down again. Forcing himself to his feet, Jinx began limping away.

The ebony samurai appeared to understand his injury, for it took up pursuit of the young hero.

Jinx hurried away as best he could but it was not in a quick manner at all. The samurai was slowly but surely gaining on him. For all its might, *it* was not particularly quick, either.

The young African had not gotten far when a loop fell about his torso, ensnaring him, and he was suddenly jerked into the air without warning.

Above him, the Crusader called down, "Just a

minute!"

In that amount of time, the two partners were reunited on the second floor of a damaged building, one wall having been knocked off, what was left of it lying scattered on the ground below in pieces.

"Thanks," said Jinx, eyeing the samurai. It charged the building, crashing into it.

Pulling his young partner along, the Crusader told him, "Time to let the cops have their turn."

Behind them, the police began a coordinated assault on the armored giant with their pistols and shotguns.

Chapter 8

## A MEETING OF MINDS

Behind police lines, the Crusader announced, "He's too much for us, I'm afraid." His voice was tinged with bitterness.

"We ain't doing so good, either," replied the cop in charge. "SWAT is on its way. We're all hoping bazookas can stop that thing."

"I'm with you," agreed the uberhero. "The Guild is convening to get involved."

"I'm glad you said that," admitted the cop. "I just got a report that there are *four* of these things in the city, scattered about. None are attacking important places you'd expect, like the Empire State Building, or Central Park. The Mayor has called a state of emergency."

The Crusader's face was grim upon digesting this news. Jinx's gaze shot back and forth between the two men, his mentor and the cop, and then the pair of uberheroes departed, returning to the waterfront where they retrieved their motorcycle, a sidecar for young Jinx attached, and drove to Guild House. They were the last to arrive, having stayed as long as possible at the battleground. The other nine members of the team were already discussing the threat, each of the four sites visible on large plasma-screen monitors in the conference room. Thompson, being their government liaison, was also present.

"Glad to see you made it back," said the Flame, peering at his old friend. Like the Crusader, he, too had started out as an apprentice to an older hero, the original Flame. Garbed in his scarlet costume with a flame emblazoned on its chest and jagged-edged boots, gloves, and collar, representing flames, he possessed his mentor's abilities to create and control fire. "These things are unbelievable."

"Anything that can be built can be destroyed," put in the Fighting Yank in an authoritative tone.

"I hope you're right," returned the Crusader. "I didn't have much of a chance against one."

"Don't feel bad," said the patriotically-themed uberhero, "You're not wearing armor."

Magno nodded to the veteran uberhero in a more convincing manner than the Fighting Yank's tone.

The Blazing Scarab announced, "This is the mystic menace I sensed last summer. It has finally surfaced."

"Does that mean you can stop it?" asked Dr. Nemesis.

"Perhaps," the Blazing Scarab answered thoughtfully. "This magic is not native to the Americas. It is foreign, comes from overseas."

"Where?" queried the Crusader. "Maybe that will give us some clue to the identity of who's behind it ... how we can *stop* him."

"I do not know," confessed the mystic. "Powerful magic hides much about these creatures."

"You mean they're not just men in armor?" the Fighting Yank asked in a surprised tone.

"Yes and no."

"I hate magic," the armored uberhero muttered.

"They are some form of man and machine merged," explained the Blazing Scarab.

"Cyborgs?" offered Dynamic Man. "I've fought

those."

"Not exactly ... not the way you mean," the Blazing Scarab clarified. "They are merged mystically, not mechanically."

"What does *that* mean?" asked Black Fury.

The Blazing Scarab replied, "I do not fully understand it. I have never before encountered such creatures. The best way I can describe it is that the creatures are composed of two parts, human and machine."

"Could they be robots controlled by a human mind via electronics?" queried Cerebex. "Could that explain their strange disparity you sense?"

"I think not.

"I am sorry I cannot explain better."

The Fighting Yank declared, "I'll take my chances with technology."

"I'd also like to try my armor against one of those," added Cerebex, who towered over all present at eight feet tall. "I was built to handle dangerous situations." A few of the members exchanged glances. No one was sure if that meant he was entirely mechanical or not. Comments the green giant made were vague, like this one, leading to speculation. No one felt comfortable broaching the topic.

"I say we give the Scarab his chance," interrupted the Crusader before the discussion got out of hand. "He knows most about what these things are ... even if it's not much. That gives him the edge."

"*Gracias*," nodded the Hispanic hero. Saying a few words in a low tone, he suddenly disappeared from sight.

Pointing to a view screen, Kitten exclaimed, "There he is!"

Indeed, the Blazing Scarab had appeared at one of the scenes. He stood there for several moments, then disappeared from sight. And then he was in the conference room again.

"What happened?" asked Magno. "We saw nothing happen."

"They are enchanted," explained the Blazing Scarab tersely. "Magic protects them from magic. I cannot stop them."

"You learned all that in under a minute?" pressed Dr. Nemesis.

Frowning, the Hispanic uberhero answered, "*Si.*

"Now I will meditate to try learn something that is useful." He then retired to one the many rooms of Guild House – the main building was equipped much like a home in certain respects, with a parlor, drawing room, library, and the like, in addition to necessities like a kitchen and formal dining room, and chambers like those of a business, offices and meeting rooms in adjacent structures.

A tension gripped the conference room. Dynamic Man broke the ice by saying, without any humor intended, "Well, that can't be good."

"I'm going to see what I can do against one of those things," the Fighting Yank announced.

"Hold on," the Crusader said, placing a hand on an armored shoulder. "Our resident mystic just told us they're too powerful for him. We can't go rushing into battle without a plan."

"That's *not* what he said," retorted the Fighting Yank. "He said *he* couldn't do anything about them. That doesn't mean *I* can't."

"My second point still stands."

"Then you stay here and plan while I see how tough one of these 'samurai' is."

"Stop," Magno interjected. "The Crusader is our elected field commander. If he says we will plan out an attack together, then that is what we will do. That is our law."

When the Fighting Yank spun on the young man, Magno told him, "I understand your feeling. I feel the same way. My staff should stop an armored man, but I see the wisdom of planning."

"We *all* want to go, Yank," added Cerebex.

"I'm not saying we have to talk about it all night," explained the Crusader in a softer tone. "Just that we coordinate our efforts rather than going off half-cocked. That's never gotten us anywhere."

"All right," the Fighting Yank said in a tight voice. "Let's get started then."

Chapter 9

## TURN OF THE SCREW

New York City's finest was fighting a losing battle, and they knew it. They'd realized it fairly quickly, as the black samurai they faced were immune to their weaponry, which had been built for anti-personnel use, not open warfare. Not only that, but the armored giants simply ignored the attacks of the cops, even the better-armed SWAT units. It had soon become apparent the police department was hopelessly outclassed by the strange armored men, who appeared to possess no weaponry of their own. They used their invulnerability to destroy Manhattan's landscape, charging into buildings and pulling down weakened sections with their armored hands. The US Army was duly called in, units arriving at the four battle sites before one AM. Their assaults began immediately.

The Army wasn't fooling around. It came with bazookas and tanks – and planes were standing by. Bombing the city was a last resort. It was now taken for granted that more damage would be done before the menace was gone – like it being darkest before the dawn, General August "Anvil" Anderson explained upon being briefed on the threat. He'd been chosen because he was known for his tenacity and his tactics: He'd earned his nickname from enemies beating themselves against his defenses until they were worn out. If ever such a strategy was needed, it was now. No offense had made a dent in the rampage of the armored figures. Perhaps the Anvil could stop them.

It was Anvil Anderson who'd pointed out that the four samurai were arranged in a rough diamond around Central Park; surely that was no coincidence. But what did it mean? No motive except wholesale destruction by the samurai was offered by experts. Any attack meant to conquer New York City would have been conducted quite differently. All the experts knew that. There was no consensus among the military strategists what the ultimate goal of the samurai was.

Old Anvil announced he did not care about motive. "Job one is stopping those things. Someone else can worry about later developments, if these things are just a first wave. They're so God-damned powerful no second wave is going to be needed, unless the purpose is to level Manhattan to its bedrock."

This claim had led to speculation that the attack had been launched by extremists, motive unknown but the goal of wiping Manhattan off the map. The experts turned their eyes toward countries that had been decimated by the US. There were a number of these in the Middle East, and more besides that held sympathies with the devastated nations. And few rogue nations such as North Korea. The Oriental flavor of the armored beings suggested a possible connection there.

Anvil Anderson left the strategists to ponder possibilities while he got on with his task.

He soon found that the samurai were as immune to his M1A2 Abrams' 150 mm M256 smoothbore guns as they were the police rifles. The tank shells were just big bullets to the four engines of destruction.

It was unbelievable.

While the ebony beings were knocked about by direct hits, they always got back up, and, after a bit, attacked the armored units of the US Army, which quickly found themselves decimated as the NYPD had been.

The battle sites were further ravaged by Anvil Anderson's attacks. Everyone expected that, and, all things considered, the damage was no worse than what the samurai had wrought in their hour-long rampage. Nothing was gained, but not much was lost in the overall scheme of things. The four sites had been evacuated by police as well as could be done under the circumstances, and some loss of civilian life was always expected in war. Delaying the Army's attack would result in greater loss of life, it had been judged, so Anvil Anderson had been given free rein.

When the results of the attacks became clear, the Anvil was on the phone with the President of the United States and the Mayor of New York City. The Governor of the state had been leapfrogged over due to the state of emergency, and while he was kept in the loop, he had no real say in anything now, much to his annoyance.

After the General had finished speaking, the President asked, "Where is the Guild?"

He had, of course, been informed of their earlier actions – in fact, Magno had been ordered to cease and desist when the Army stepped in.

The Mayor said, "They have some new information about the samurai and are planning a strategy based on that."

"Did they bother to share this?" the President asked angrily.

"Well, sir," explained the Mayor, "the machines are *magical*. The Guild is uncertain the samurai can be defeated by mere force and are attempting to find a magical solution."

The President of the United States was speechless at this pronouncement.

## Chapter 10

## FIRE POWER

The plan that developed among Guild members was to split into pairs – there were four of these, not counting Jinx, who was still a junior member and could always be found at the Crusader's side, and the Blazing Scarab had removed himself from any possible fight so he could try to learn something useful mystically – just as there were four black samurai. While this would seem an easy task to assign partners, it was not. Black Fury would not work with the Fighting Yank due to political differences, he being a staunch love-it-or-leave-it conservative and she being a diversity-propounding liberal. She also would not work with Magno, for he was Japanese and she Chinese and the Chinese had not forgotten Nanking, nor forgiven it.

The Crusader, being field commander of the Guild, paired her with Cerebex, whom everyone liked. His plan was to pair a weaker uberhero with a stronger one, so that the couples were generally of similar power level; two lesser-powered members would stand no chance against one of the black samurai. Kitten went with Magno, while Dynamic Man was paired with the Fighting Yank. This left the Flame and Dr. Nemesis with the Crusader, while Jinx was assigned the task of staying in Guild House as liaison and contact, since he was still nursing a limp.

The young man did not object.

"I'm glad you're with me, Crusader," confided the Flame as his group departed Guild House. The two were old friends, both having been teen sidekicks to uberheroes of the first generation: The first Flame and Crusader, and Dr. Nemesis, who made everyone around him feel small.

"We have as much of a chance as any other group," supplied the living titan. "You did a good job pairing us up."

"Thanks, Doc," returned the Crusader. Only he and the Flame, due to their long association with him, had the temerity to call him this familiarly. The original Flame had appeared the same year as Nemesis, and the Crusader the following year. 2006 had been the year of the "beta human", men and women who possessed "uber powers" or "uberpowers" – what was called in the comic books "superpowers". 2007 was then the year of the "uberhero" ("uber wealthy" already being in use at the time); the Crusader had been the first to wear an actual costume, and shortly the Flame had followed suit, inspired by his lead. Dr. Nemesis remained in plainclothes, he'd explained to the others, to avoid making himself a target. Not all beta humans wore costumes and not all uberheroes had uber*powers*.

Spark – young Roddy Corcoran – had joined the Flame the year after he'd debuted. It had been at his suggestion that his idol the Flame had donned a distinctive costume – the one Roddy wore now as the second Flame. He was the first "legacy" hero, literally, having inherited not only the identity of the Flame, but his uber powers, as well.

The ubervillain Blitz seemed as fast as his

namesake – "blitz" was German for "lightning". Sparks flew as he evaded the Flame's fire bursts, for an aura of electricity surrounded him, protecting him from the elements – or anything untoward that came his way that was solid.

He zipped up to the Flame and slugged him on the chin, shooting off more sparks. The uberhero fought back – he knew how to brawl, having done so around the world in his many explorations. But he was no match for electrified punches. He shot flames from his fingertips. Blitz sped away, and, before the Flame knew it, had come up behind him. Placing his hands about the uberhero's neck, he began choking him, simultaneously electrocuting him.

"Sparky", as the young *Spark* was called, jumped on Blitz from behind. He struggled to remove him from his mentor but the strength of the nineteen year-old was no match for the electrically-enhanced might of the ubervillain. He was simply and plainly ignored.

Realizing he couldn't pull Blitz free, Sparky stepped back and gave the ubervillain's knee a good kick. His body dipped but he did not fall; nor did he release his victim. He kicked back, catching Sparky by surprise, sending voltage through him with the unexpected blow. Stunned, the teenager fell to the street. He fought unconsciousness and crawled toward his faltering mentor.

Suddenly, the Flame seemed to explode in a sunburst.

When Sparky regained his sight, both men lay on the ground, Blitz's body burned black. The Flame was still conscious when Sparky reached him. He lay still, his eyes dim.

"This is the end, kid," the Flame told Sparky, his voice weak and faltering. "I know it …."

The young man said, "No, don't – "

"Nothing I can do about it .... I'll be gone before medics get here," rasped the Flame. "But there is one thing ... I can do .... I can give you the *power*...."

"I'm not worthy, Pat," Sparky declared with tears in his eyes.

The Flame choked out a laugh, blood sputtering from his lips.

"Worthy?" he rasped. "You mean that story about only those worthy of wielding the fire power can summon it? That was just some bullshit I made up to impress other uberheroes, Roddy ... the Crusader was just some average Joe who had the balls to fight guys who outclassed him, and Dr. Nemesis ... well, he's *Dr. Nemesis*. He makes everyone else feel inadequate, including me.

"What I'm trying to tell you is ... anyone can summon the fire power with the right training."

"But ...."

"The masters of the city liked me, so they taught the trick to me. I don't know how to teach it, or I would have taught you, Roddy. I can do it but I can't teach it.

"I can't *teach* it to you but I can *give* it to you .... I ...." The Flame's voice trailed off.

A bright amorphous flame seemed to rise from the Flame as he went limp with death, and before Sparky could react – he stared in silent awe – the thing enveloped him and disappeared, and he knew that he now had the power.

## Chapter 11

## 2x2 AND 4x4

"Jesus," murmured Dynamic Man, upon arriving at one of the four battle sites in Manhattan. The Fighting Yank was carrying him by his arms over the city, the young man refusing to be carried like a baby in his armored arms. "I've never seen anything like this ... except in old photos in History class. This looks like bombed-out cities from WW II."

The pair landed not far from the black samurai. On his own two feet again, Dynamic Man asked, "How do you want to do this? Do you want to attack together or split up ...?"

"I'll handle this," declared the Fighting Yank, without turning to look at his young companion.

"Be my guest," Dynamic Man told him. "You're the veteran here."

"You're usually the one to rush into things. Scared?"

"Realistic," countered the young redheaded uberhero tartly. "I know I don't have much of a chance against that thing but I'll stand by to back you up if you need it since you want to go in alone. I can provide a great distraction."

"*If* I need it ...."

"You know, you're kind of an asshole," observed Dynamic Man in a rueful tone.

"Just confident in my abilities," returned the

armored uberhero easily as he rose once more into the air, propelled by a powerful backpack rocket assembly.

"No," murmured Dynamic Man. "The consensus is asshole."

The navy-blue armor with red-and-white-striped limbs was the most advanced weapons system in existence. From the air, the Fighting Yank shot invisible beams of fire – charged particle beams that could melt a jet in flight.

The armored giant reacted immediately – by turning and running away, taking refuge in what remained of a nearby building. The man inside the red-white-and-blue armor smiled.

Out of a corner of an eye, the Fighting Yank saw Dynamic Man waving his arms. But above the roar of the rockets, he could not hear what he was shouting. When the young uberhero pointed at the demolished structure, the Fighting Yank, nodded that he knew where the black samurai had gone.

An urgent beeping indicated a collision was imminent – but the floating suit of armor wasn't moving, it was stationary in the air, hovering in place while the Fighting Yank searched for the samurai.

Staley caught sight of the armored giant falling toward him from above a moment too late to act. The samurai had raced up above him, hidden from view by the building, and jumped down at him!

The Fighting Yank sped away – too late! The black samurai rammed into his waist, and grappled with the armored uberhero as he flew away. The armor, as sophisticated as it was, could not compensate for the sudden new weight quickly. The pair spiraled for a few moments before straightening out on a course toward the ground!

Dynamic Man was in motion before the grappling

pair impacted.

The collision with the street was forceful enough to rattle already damaged structures nearby. Under the black samurai, the Fighting Yank fired his CPB weapon again. The armored giant grabbed hold of the offending arm and squeezed. The delicate device crumpled under the pressure, and imploded, damaging the armor and the arm inside it.

The samurai didn't wait for another attack to begin. He yanked on the uberhero's arm, trying to pull it off.

From the roof of a parked car – it was demolished now, and nothing more than junk – Dynamic Man unclipped one of the golden discs on his costume at strategic locations and threw it with unerring accuracy. It struck the armored giant. Though it did not damage the samurai, it hesitated – for just a moment.

Not out of the fight, the Fighting Yank lifted his legs, pointed the soles of his boots at the black giant, and kicked. This sent the engine of destruction a few yards away. The armored uberhero quickly rolled over. When the black samurai came at him again, the Fighting Yank bent over and fired his rocket pack at it. The blast sent the two armored beings in opposite directions. The patriotically-armored uberhero was in the air before the samurai was back on its feet. He quickly launched himself back into the air.

As he passed overhead, the Fighting Yank uberhero dipped down and scooped up Dynamic Man with his good arm, telling him, "I think my arm's not too badly damaged but I'm out of the fight. We're going to have to retreat unless you want a crack at that thing."

Seeing the expression on his young colleague's face, he added, "You don't have to say it. I was overconfident. But I learn from my mistakes."

The young uberhero replied tartly, "You're welcome."


"Why don't you stay back, at least until I can assess the situation," Cerebex suggested to Black Fury. "I was built for this sort of thing."

"I will follow you in, just in case," replied the uberheroine.

"Have it your way …. But be careful." There was almost a paternal tone to the electronic voice of the armored giant. Everyone assumed a man was ensconced within the metal suit. The personality *seemed* male. Even the artificial electronic voice was keyed low like a male's. The few times it had referred to itself, Black Fury seemed to recall, it had been a "he".

There had been conjecture among Guild members about this – gossip. The name "Cerebex" reminded certain members of the cerebrum, the large part of the brain that contained the cerebral cortex, which was responsible for cognition, playing a key role in attention, perception, awareness, thought, memory, language, and consciousness. The cerebrum was also responsible for sensory processing, speech, and learning. Could "Cerebex" be a contraction of "cerebrum-x", "X" as in "experimental" as they used in new aircraft? No one had thought to ask Cerebrex when he'd joined if he was a person – or an artificial intelligence. It seemed both an invasion of privacy now, and too late to bring up the subject since he had served well since joining in 2021, and had been a member of the Guild in good standing all that time.

Without a glance back, Cerebex trundled off in the direction of the samurai, having cleared the police line with his partner some minutes earlier. He soon came upon his target, as Black Fury, several yards behind, took up a vantage point from which to observe – watching for signs of weakness. She practiced Wing Chun, a form of kung fu that emphasized offense.

"Cease and desist," Cerebex called out. This got the attention of the ebony-armored figure if nothing else. The smooth, featureless helmet hid whatever its wearer felt, giving no sign of any emotion at all.

It did not pause to study the newcomer, but marched toward the green giant, which towered over the tall samurai, ready to fight. Cerebex raised his blocky arms, pointed his fingers at the oncoming armored figure and shot arcs of electricity at it.

Seeing this assault had no effect on the samurai, the giant murmured in a clinical tone, "Hmm. Must be insulated like me."

In response to the attack, the black samurai leaped the remaining distance, and landed on Cerebex, toppling the green giant. It began pummeling Cerebex with its fists. He reached up, and, grasping the samurai by the head, plucked him off the green armor.

"I'm built better than that," Cerebex informed the black samurai.

The ebony-armored figure tore himself loose from Cerebex's grip, and, falling back down upon the supine giant, attacked an arm. It damaged the limb, crippling it, before the green giant could stop it. It then went to work on the other arm.

Though the limb was pinned by the samurai's might, unable to break free, its fingers elongated into tentacles – metal cables hidden within each forearm. These quickly ensnared the black figure, and pulled it away.

Cerebex's chest opened, revealing a projector that fired a bright concussion ray, that, timed with the movement of his tentacles like machine guns and propellers on early airplanes, blasted the ebony samurai, knocking him a dozen yards away.

"Stay back!" the green giant called to Black Fury. "He's too much! Fall back!"

Reluctantly, the Chinese uberheroine complied.

As the tentacles retracted into place, Cerebex pointed his palm at the rising samurai, and bathed him in flames. The ebony-armored figure seemed not to notice these as he lurched toward the green giant.

Having exhausted his array of weapons and come up short, Cerebex rose into the air, his feet flaring with rocket power, and retreated.

As he landed behind the police line where Black Fury, the young Chinese woman, seeing the ruined arm, asked, "Are you all right?"

"I'm fine ... just a flesh wound, my dear," answered Cerebex idly, his mind obviously elsewhere.


Upon seeing the devastation in person, Kitten, who was crouched low, purred, "We're not in Kansas anymore, Toto."

Rather sharply, Magno, standing straight beside her, asked, "Why do you call me that?"

"Because," Kitten responded in a puzzled tone, "it's a saying ... a quote from the 'Wizard of Oz'. You know ... the *movie?* Dorothy and her dog Toto?"

"I do not, sorry," confessed Magno. "What does it mean?"

"We're in a new and totally foreign situation. For me, it reminded me of coming to America ... how different it is than Iran."

"You are an immigrant?" queried the young

Japanese-American.

"My parents," answered Kitten. "They told me stories of Iran before and after the 1979 revolution. I was born here."

"I see."

"Why did calling you Toto upset you?"

"That is what my *friends* call me ...."

In a polite tone, Magno said to Kitten, "No offense intended. Being of a superior intelligence, I never had many friends my own age. It was not that you are not my friend, but my concern was that you had somehow deduced my civilian identity."

"How many young Japanese-American geniuses are there in this city?" Kitten queried. "But, no, I don't know it. It never occurred to me try to find out. My nickname's Balikabaja, so now we're even."

"What does that mean? Another dog name?"

The young Muslim grinned. "It means 'kitten' in Arabic."

Not finding the humor in this, Magno said, "If I may, I think it would be best to allow me to attack first. If I am correct, my staff should be able to end this threat."

"I hope so," said the young uberheroine. "There's not much I can do against something like that."

"Just so. I sense this is all metal – *kikai*, a machine ... robot," Magno murmured as his staff lifted him into the air by manipulating the Earth's magnetic field.

Kitten looked at her companion. Not much anxiety showed on her brown face, and Magno seemed not to have noticed anything amiss, his attention focused on the engine of destruction before them. Then, quietly, he told her, "I will not tell anyone."

Speechless, Kitten watched Magno as he floated

toward the giant black samurai, holding the crooked staff in both hands. Girders among the debris came to life, and wrapped themselves around the armored figure. These were still winding themselves about the black samurai when it began unwrapping itself, pulling the girders into long ribbons of steel. This went on for some time, with neither gaining the upper hand. All Magno accomplished was keeping the engine of destruction busy, so that it could cause no more deadly carnage.

Frowning, the Japanese uberhero changed his tack. He directed his power *at* the armored giant. Its skin began to warp – then unbelievably, like a wave passing, the metal smoothed back to its normal shape, and remained that way.

"That is not normal," he observed quietly as he returned to his partner's side.

Kitten offered: "Blazing Scarab told us they were magic."

"Of course."

The two uberheroes exchanged tense glances.

"I seem to be powerless to stop it," confessed Magno.

"But you can *delay* it," offered Kitten. "You can stop it from killing more people and doing more damage.

"You just keep doing that, if you can, and I'll report in."

"I will ... and thank you."

Magno once again floated gently into the night sky and began summoning all the metal he could find nearby.


Electric blue eyes below close-cropped platinum blond hair surveyed the devastation caused by the rampage of the samurai. Dr. Nemesis murmured, "My God ...."

"Yeah," agreed the Crusader, beside him, still astonished by the carnage.

The Flame looked on in silence, coolly appraising the scene emotionlessly.

Removing his suit jacket, revealing an uberhuman physique in a tight short-sleeved tunic, Nemesis cracked his knuckles. He glanced casually at the Crusader, and said, "I'd like a shot at him."

"He's all yours, Doc," returned the uberhero. "I know I don't have to tell you to be careful."

With a grunt, Dr. Nemesis picked his way through the debris, working his way to the ebony samurai. His jaw was set. No fear showed on his handsome face. He was the most powerful being on planet Earth and had yet to meet his physical match in his eighteen years as a professional adventurer and crime fighter.

Once he had cleared the major obstacles between him and the ebony engine of destruction, Nemesis charged the samurai. The two collided with an enormous impact that sounded like a bomb had gone off.

On the ground, the two fought, throwing punches that could sink battleships. Nemesis was surprised to find the armored figure resisted his might – it showed on his face for just a moment, then he redoubled his efforts. But no matter what he did, the samurai would not fall. And though the armored giant was no stronger than the first uberhuman, he was implacable. Nothing seemed to hurt him, not even Dr. Nemesis' full strength. The samurai was pummeling his foe into unconsciousness.

"Holy shit!" exclaimed the Crusader. "Doc is going down!"

There seemed little doubt of it now. Nemesis was slowing, not able to fend off every blow of the ebony samurai. He got in no counter punches, did not even make the attempt many times.

Stepping away from his old friend, the Flame formed and threw a fireball over the battling pair's head, where it exploded like Independence Day fireworks. This got the armored giant's attention – at least momentarily.

Creating a thermal updraft, the Flame rose into the night sky, looking like a firefly from a distance, then powerful blasts flew from his downward-pointing hands, propelling him rapidly toward the embattled pair like a rocket.

The Crusader moved to take advantage of his friend's ploy. Moving quickly but stealthily, he headed for the stunned Dr. Nemesis, who was moving feebly on the street.

Overhead, the Flame drifted toward the ebony samurai, which fruitlessly grabbed up at the fiery being. Seeing this tactic useless, it bent, picked up a large bit of debris and hurled it at the Flame – who flitted aside.

Flames spurted from the fingertips of the uberhero, quickly engulfing the armored giant and turning him into a living pyre. Red hot, it began thrashing about in silence. But not in pain – in *frustration*, renewing its rampage of destruction.

Seeing the Crusader had gotten Dr. Nemesis to safety, the Flame retreated. When he reached his two teammates, he declared, "Either that armor has the best insulation in the world or there's nothing alive inside it – it's a robot."

Nemesis, propped up by the Crusader as he regained his senses, announced in a weak voice, "Fighting these things this way is pointless. We're going to have to find another way ... they're too powerful to fight hand-to-hand."

If anyone knew the veracity of such a claim, it was the world's first beta human.

## Chapter 12

## TRUTH, LIKE AN ONION

No matter how much Magno threw at the black samurai, it kept on coming. But his erstwhile partner had been correct: At least it wasn't killing people anymore.

When he had finally succeeded in burying it beneath a mound of debris – the remains of several automobiles – Kitten came to the armored uberhero, and told him, "You're doing better than the other teams. They all failed .... They had to retreat."

"I feel that I have failed," confessed the young Japanese uberhero.

With the grinding noise of metal against metal, the armored giant emerged from the anthill-like mound.

"How can it survive all this?" Kitten purred.

"It apparently survived falling from the sky," answered Magno. "It may be unstoppable."

"So let's not try to stop it."

Before Magno could respond, the ebony samurai picked up the wreckage of an automobile and threw it at the pair of uberheroes. It stopped suddenly, mid air, held aloft by the armored uberhero's electronic staff.

"Quickly," Magno snapped. "What do you mean?"

"Why don't you throw him into the East River?" Kitten suggested. This was the river nearest their location on the West Side.

"I am ashamed that I did not think of it," Magno said as he manipulated his staff, causing the black samurai to rise into the air, where it flailed like a fish out of water.

As he rose, the armored uberhero said to Kitten, "Come on." Then she, too, followed him into the air, and the pair trailed the black samurai west. Once it was over the East River, Magno dropped the thing in. With a splash, it abruptly sank from sight. The main channel of the river was forty feet to the bottom.

Floating above the river, the two uberheroes watched for the black samurai. Her lithe form tense, Kitten showed some anxiety at being suspended mid air. Long minutes passed.

"Your plan seems to have worked," announced Magno. "Well done."

"In my job I have to work smart. Brute force won't get the job done," Kitten explained.

"And what might that be?"

With a grin, she replied, "Oh, no, you don't, Toto."

Frowning, Magno said, "Do not reveal that to anyone."

"Of course not," Kitten said seriously. "I was only joking." Magno was known among Guild members for being humorless.

Then, noise from behind the floating pair caught their attention. The black samurai, covered in river mud, was climbing up onto shore.

"Nothing will stop it." Magno said grimly.

"He's like a Terminator!" Kitten muttered.

If the Japanese uberhero caught this reference, he did not mention it.

Suddenly, the Blazing Scarab was beside the pair. Kitten hissed at him: "Never sneak up on a cat!"

Nodding, the mystic said, "Apologies. I have come to bring you back to Guild House, where we are about to plan a new strategy."

"Can we use it now?" queried Magno.

"No ... I have news that may help inform our next move. These 'robots' are not mere machines. Their creator has mystically merged magic and machine .... In some way that still eludes me, he has imbued these machines with life.

"Admittedly, I have not been active long, but I possess a vast storehouse of mystic lore, and I have not heard of such a thing. I do not know how to overcome such a thing. That is why we are meeting again – the other teams failed, and perhaps with this revelation, a new strategy will come to us."

"I am going to stay here and mitigate as much destruction as possible," Magno announced.

"As you wish," the Blazing Scarab nodded. Turning to Kitten the mystic said, "Take my hand, child, and we will return to Guild House."

The young uberheroine did so, and the two disappeared from sight.

## Chapter 13

## THE WRECKING CREW

"You're pretty handy with that," Cerebex's buzzing electronic voice told the Fighting Yank as he finished welding a patch on the damaged limb of the green giant.

"I have to be able to make field repairs," replied the armored uberhero. He had replaced his own damaged sleeve, and was favoring the arm a bit. After a moment, he observed, "Those are pretty advanced electronics there ...."

"I'd need them for a modern suit of armor – "

"I don't mean to pry, but it doesn't look to me like there's much room in there for a human."

"There is no human in the armor, no human at risk," explained Cerebex. "I was built to protect humans."

"Are you a robot with an independent AI?" the Fighting Yank asked in a concerned tone.

"That would worry all of you, wouldn't it?" the green giant asked in a grave tone.

"I know we didn't ask when we *recruited* you ... no one thought to. Not even me ...."

"You *did* recruit me," said Cerebex, "and I never lied to you. But I *am* human, and I am in here ... and if you'll keep this to yourself, I'm not normal sized. I'm a dwarf. I fit nicely in the torso. That's one reason the frame is so large, so I'm not cramped in the chest compartment."

"Ah," mused the Fighting Yank.

"Another reason is, I probably built Cerebex oversized to compensate for my diminutive size. I was just joking with you about being a robot ... to hide clues to my identity. How many genius dwarves are there in this city? In the *country?* It probably wouldn't be too hard to find me if one were really looking."

"Thank you," the armored hero said sincerely, "but you didn't need to tell me all of that. I only wanted to know that you weren't an AI. We've all seen what mistakes they can make, and there could be repercussions since an AI doesn't have any legal rights."

"I know it wasn't idle curiosity," Cerebex told his fellow Guild member. "I know you're looking out for the team. No hard feelings.

"Now that temporary repairs are finished, shall we join the others in the war room?"


The main conference room – formerly the main hall of the townhouse – was sometimes called the "war room" because it was the nerve center of the Guild's crime-fighting operation, where strategy and tactics in their war on crime were planned. Everyone else had gathered there after their unsuccessful attacks on the four samurai to compare notes and plan a new strategy after learning the engines of destruction were more powerful than they'd assumed. It was not often the Guild had suffered such humiliating defeats in their four-year history. But the first battle did not always decide the war.

The remaining eight members of the Guild – not all of whom were active members, but this was an emergency, an all hands on deck situation – were watching the rampages of the samurai on oversized plasma screens.

It looked like war.

The devastation was unbelievable, worse than 9-11 because it was more widespread – and occurring at four locations, not just one.

"How are we going to stop this?" Black Fury asked of no one in particular in a subdued tone.

Thompson offered, "There are rumors that the President is considering an experimental weapon that's top secret."

"Until, then, this is Blazing Scarab's show," announced Dr. Nemesis. "He sensed it a year ago, and he found out that magic and machine are connected somehow in these samurai. What do you say, Scarab?"

"*Lo siento*," said the Hispanic hero. "I am not familiar with this technology ... or even this type of magic. It is foreign to me."

"I didn't know that magic was different from place to place," returned the living titan. "Perhaps you know an Oriental mage?" The Crusader and Nemesis had both agreed there was an Oriental cast to the features of the samurai.

"Why do you ask?"

"Crusader said it was samurai," answered the Fighting Yank.

"It's Japanese," supplied Dr. Nemesis. "Why?"

"I wish someone had told me earlier," the mage said in a tight voice. "I would have investigated Oriental magic as the source. Now I shall.

"And I do not know any other sorcerers," confessed the Blazing Scarab. "As you know, I have not been active long."

Nemesis gave him an encouraging smile. "For all we know, you'd been studying or even operating quietly for a decade before you joined us …. That ghost-breaker Douglas Drew tries to stay out of headlines …."

Few present had heard of the man, but no one was surprised Dr. Nemesis had. He was a living encyclopedia, despite possessing no higher education; he'd learned what he knew living life, not sitting in a classroom or library. He even resided in a former museum uptown, now full of trophies he'd collected on his global adventures. He had been active for almost twenty years, the world's first beta human, starting out as an explorer and adventurer. When he'd run across international crime in his travels, he added "crime fighter" to his resumé.

Some saw him as the *superman* the philosopher Friedrich Nietzsche had predicted in *Thus Spoke Zarathustra*, published in 1883. While hailed as embodying the ideals of the Nazi regime, the philosopher was in reality opposed to anti-Semitism and nationalism, going so far as to call for all anti-Semites to be shot dead.

"Armed with this new knowledge, I must return to my sanctuary and search for a means to stop these unholy creatures," announced the Blazing Scarab. "I have exhausted all my resources here."

"I'd like to get a look at it some time," Dr. Nemesis said.

Without answering, the mystic stepped through time and space to his hidden temple in Mexico, disappearing from view in an instant.

## Chapter 14

## THE BIG SHOT

A handful of men joined the President of the United States in the living quarters in the White House. Dressed like men who been roused in the middle of the night, they were all white, and it was fair to call them "old"; their ages were between sixty years of age and eighty. With one exception, a young man whose demeanor and dress screamed "security".

The meeting was not on any official calendar, though of course the names of the attendees were on the list of those to be admitted to the White House. Those in charge of security knew the men's names as personal friends of the President. They were members of his "Kitchen Cabinet". This term came from 1832 to describe Andrew Jackson's private advisors after his purge of the official cabinet and his break with Vice President Calhoun. It had been coined by the President's political enemies, and was not meant to be flattering. Now it was part of Washington's everyday politics.

Not being composed of capitol bigwigs and taking place in the residence, the meeting was classified as "personal", rather than "official", and no record was kept of the meeting. The President did not need to swear its attendees to secrecy: He trusted them.

There was one man present, one of the "youngsters" in their sixties, whom no one recognized

– except the President. He had never attended earlier meetings of the group. Once everyone had arrived, POTUS introduced him as, "Stanford Hope, ballistics expert and military historian. Dr. Hope ...."

The gray-templed bespectacled man set his phone on a small plastic stand he had brought with him and placed upon a table, and suddenly an image was sprayed onto a white wall. Pictured was a very big artillery gun, its barrel 150 feet long.

The weathered faces of the men in the parlor frowned and their eyes squinted at the photo, for its content was unfamiliar to them.

The President told those assembled, "General Anderson has reported that his weaponry has been ineffective against the four robots in New York. So we need something *bigger* ...."

"What *is* that thing?" asked one of the men. "I've never seen anything like it."

"Have any of you heard of the 'Big Shot'?" asked Hope.

No one answered.

But one man finally said in a tentative voice, "Isn't that one of Bull's superguns?"

Nodding, Hope explained to the others, "Gerald Bull was a Canadian engineer who developed very long range artillery. These became known as 'superguns'. He worked for CADRE – Canadian Artillery Development Research Establishment, and an installation was built at a military training and artillery range just outside of Quebec City in the early Sixties."

"If this thing has been around for sixty years, why hasn't any of us heard of it?" asked another attendee.

"You'll probably recognize later parts of the story," the President broke in. "*I* did."

Hope continued. "Bull's work was part of Project

HARP – High Altitude Research Project."

"I've heard of that," offered another fellow. "It's that weather control facility."

"That's HAARP with two 'As'," Hope corrected, unperturbed by his audience's ignorance. "Different project.

"Testing with the first guns began in 1965 and into 1966. The US became interested, and we started our own program, setting up a facility in Yuma, Arizona, while Bull had one built on Barbados. These are the only three of these in existence."

"I still don't recognize any of this," complained one of the men who had spoken earlier.

"Bull later went to work for Iraq, and was murdered in 1990," Hope said.

"Oh, yes," exclaimed another attendee. "I recall the name now. Assassinated by MOSSAD, wasn't he?"

"It's very likely," Stanford Hope conceded, though this wasn't his area of expertise.

There followed a discussion of Bull, Iraq, and his death, until the President interrupted. "*Gentlemen* …."

"Quebec lies 440 miles away as the crows flies," said Hope. "The range of the Big Shot is 465 miles."

A moment of silence followed, until the group of men grasped the implication. One said, "You can't mean – "

"We are running out of options," POTUS said in a grave tone. "We can shell the city or nuke it. Or …."

"You think this is the least devastating option?"

"I do, based on Dr. Hope's data," answered the President.

"One strike in Central Park will encompass the four sites of the robots," explained the ballistic expert.

"It's a large target that will be easy to hit. Aiming such a big gun is something that has been solved to some degree since Bull worked on them, but it's still not precise.

"By contrast, shelling from a ship or dropping bombs is less precise. Much of the city will be unnecessarily destroyed due to imprecise strikes by these methods. And, in my opinion, even a small nuclear bomb is out of the question."

"The decision to be made is," interjected the President, "use the Big Shot or keep throwing conventional weaponry at it."

"What about the Guild? I heard they got involved," said one of the attendees.

"They failed," POTUS announced solemnly.

Blazing Scarab stepped back into normal space-time inside Guild House. Having been expected, no alarms went off. He announced to the assembled membership of the Guild, "As you know, I am prevented from *damaging* the mystical machines due to magical protection. This also prevents *you* from doing permanent damage to them. This is why Magno could temporarily bend one out of shape, but could not tear it apart. I believe the solution is that brute force is doomed to fail, while what you call a surgical strike may prove effective. That is to say, rather than trying to stop the creature, try to break through its armor.

"I propose the most powerful of us train our might on *one* of the living machines."

## Chapter 15

## DARK WIND

Cerebex, Magno, the Fighting Yank, Dr. Nemesis, and Blazing Scarab traveled to the nearest battleground, not far east of Guild House near the East River, close to the United Nations buildings. The mystic transported them in a disorienting journey that took just a moment. As soon as he caught sight of the ebony samurai, he began chanting in a tongue not heard for centuries, the language of the ancient Olmecs. Unlike spell casting in certain fiction, the magical cant was not spoken in rhyme.

After a few moments, the Blazing Scarab announced, "It resists me. I cannot affect it at all. This is powerful magic." He gestured to Magno with a hand. The armored uberhero manipulated his short-handled crooked staff, and those with him saw the black skin of the samurai begin to bend and bulge as if it had suddenly grown boils. These roiled along its metal surface.

The Fighting Yank took to the air, flying close enough to apply his high-energy charged particle beam. Being invisible, the only evidence of its presence was a spot on the ebony armor that bulged outward heating to a bright red.

As the engine of destruction attempted to flee the assault upon it, Dr. Nemesis leaped to it, and took hold of it, keeping it in place for the Fighting Yank.

Cerebex joined his colleague, entrapping its legs with his finger tentacles.

The samurai sought to tear itself free from the grip of Nemesis, who possessed the strength of two hundred men. It was no stronger, and, grappling rather than fighting hand to hand, the invulnerability that had given it the advantage in its first combat with the living titan was useless now. Now it was simply might against might.

The Fighting Yank's CPB jigged across the bulge in the armor created by Magno's staff. The superheated spot silently exploded like a multi-colored firework, and the samurai collapsed in Dr. Nemesis' arms. He held it for a few moments to make certain it wasn't faking. Then he dropped it and stepped away from it. It did not move.

As the Fighting Yank landed beside the fallen samurai, Nemesis took its helmet in his hands, and wrenched it loose. It came off easily now.

Training his ice-blue eyes upon the mystic, Dr. Nemesis called out, "Scarab! Get over here!"

An instant later, the Blazing Scarab stood beside the living titan. He was speechless when he gazed at the armored creature. It possessed no head. The armor was empty.


"*Do yatte?!*" spat the Claw in ancient Japanese as he saw the samurai fall. He'd watched the fight in a cloud of mist that hovered before his face, providing him with a 3-dimensional view of the battlefield. "*Doshite kono yona sonzai-tachi ga watashi no samurai o taosu koto ga dekita nodeshou ka?!*" – How could these beings have defeated my samurai?!

Turning to the dark-suited men who stood behind him, at the ready to obey, the demon said, "Begin making more samurai. After snuffing out this city like a candle, we will move to the nation's capital, and my dark wind will continue there."

"Yes, master," answered the two of the men present in one voice before they turned to obey.

The Blazing Scarab silently studied the defunct armor at Dr. Nemesis' feet.

"It doesn't look like it was even built to hold a human," observed the Fighting Yank.

"*Si*," agreed the Latin mystic. "It was not. The synthesis of life and machine I sensed was a soul of the dead trapped within. Piercing the armor freed it."

"My God, that's monstrous," mouthed Nemesis.

Standing, he told the trio of uberheroes, "Now that you know what to do, can you apply this to the remaining three creatures?"

"Of course," said the Fighting Yank.

"What will you be doing, Scarab?" inquired Nemesis.

"I will attempt to locate the source of this magic, now that I have a clue to its origin," answered the mystic as he stepped through time and space.

"I hate it when he does that," pronounced the armored uberhero.

"Let's collect Magno and be on our way," Dr. Nemesis said grimly.

The remaining members of the Guild in their headquarters were cheering, having seen the defeat of the black samurai on a view screen. The mood dampened when Thompson entered the chamber – having slipped out unnoticed minutes earlier – and announced, "I just informed my superiors that you've found a way to stop the samurai, and they informed me that they can't reach the President. He's been in a meeting discussing his options. I can tell you from professional experience that this is not good news. He's considering a last resort weapon."

"You mean a tactical nuke?" the Crusader queried.

"Probably not," said the security liaison. "But the damage won't be much short of that. If anyone has any favors to call in to get through to the President before the weapon is used, now's the time to do it."

## Chapter 16

## THE TWO EVILS

The Blazing Scarab appeared in Guild House while his teammates made their way toward the next nearest samurai. Needing to meditate, he'd stepped into one of the quiet rooms in the headquarters. There were a few of these, from a parlor to a drawing room to a study to a library to a lounge. The differences between these labels bordered on semantics at times. The parlor was for receiving guests in the secure area of the main building; the foyer complex, which included a reception desk, coat room, and restroom, was open to visitors, but only those who were deemed not to be a threat were allowed into the secure zone that described the remainder of the main building. The great drawing room was adjacent to the parlor, and used as an interview room frequently, and beyond it, a hidden smaller drawing room that was used for, among other things, observing the great drawing room; it accessed the hallway outside. The library and study were similarly grouped together. Members sometimes read in either room. The lounge was specifically for relaxing, but could get quite noisy with conversation and card playing and the like.

The Blazing Scarab had chosen the small withdrawing room, since it was least likely to be occupied. He was still going into a meditative state when the Crusader burst into the chamber. He said,

"It's a good thing our alarm system works, or we wouldn't even know you'd returned."

"I am making progress on the individual behind these inhuman creatures," explained the mystic wearily, "and was about to attempt to locate him based on new information I received that he is probably Asian."

"Something more urgent's come up, Scarab."

In a curious tone, the Hispanic hero said, "Oh?"

The Crusader explained what he'd learned about the President and some sort of super weapon that would devastate the city. "We don't have any way to get through to him. Can you *take* us there?"

The Blazing Scarab nodded, rising to his feet. "Of course. A few minutes' delay will not do any harm to my own quest. Let us go."


The men in the White House residence of the President jumped at the sudden appearance of the senior members of the Guild – the Crusader, the Flame – and, of course, the Blazing Scarab.

One of the men moved to summon Secret Service agents. The Latino mystic's scarab glowed as it froze him in place.

"No need to be alarmed, Mr. President," the Crusader said. "It's really us. We have an important message for you. *Don't use the super weapon you're considering* – the other members of our team have defeated one of the samurai and are now engaging a second. They should all be stopped within the hour if our luck holds."

"H-how did you know about the Big Shot?" stammered POTUS.

"We wouldn't be the Guild if we didn't," the Flame returned coolly.

Glancing at his aide – the man who had gone for the alarm – the aged President nodded, and the fellow brought a phone to the Chief Executive. "This is the President," he said into the secure landline telephone. "Stand down. I repeat: Stand down."

"Thank you," said the Crusader.

Then the trio of heroes disappeared as suddenly as they'd arrived, leaving members of the kitchen cabinet with their mouths still open.

His eyes closing as he put himself into a trance, the Blazing Scarab allowed his mystic senses to expand out of the drawing room, out of the townhouse, out into the city until he perceived all of Manhattan. He found a number of "bright" spots around the city, but few *large* bright spots. He was looking for one thing: foreign magic – *Oriental* magic. He ignored the two "blips" of the remaining samurai, and focused on a *source* of magic – not its product.

The Hispanic hero started, his eyes snapping open, at the power of it when he finally located it, though he shouldn't have. Trapping souls and using them to animate armor was far beyond the reach of most practitioners. Whoever was at work was no ordinary mage.

Standing, the Blazing Scarab hied himself to the location of the powerful sorcerer. He appeared on the sidewalk, stumbling and falling to one knee at the surface of the building there as if he's stumbled into it while walking. A mystic shield had repelled his entrance!

Focusing the might of his blazing scarab, the mystic forced his way inside, silently rending the shield to admit him using the physical force application of his scarab that functioned like psychokineses, which allowed the Hispanic uberhero to fly, among other things; then he appeared in the penthouse where his quarry awaited, stepping through time and space. The Scarab found an old Asian, flanked by younger Asians in dark suits. He sensed evil emanating from each of them, but the old man's aura eclipsed those of the younger men, who were now drawing heavy automatics from their armpits.

A frail hand raised by the old man stopped them. He studied the Blazing Scarab in silence.

The Latino mystic said, "What are you? I sense you are not *human* ...."

Slowly, the old man gripped his flesh and began peeling it away to reveal a monstrous abomination underneath, greater in size than his human shell had been. In Japanese, the Claw said, "I do not know your kind."

Using his scarab to translate, the Hispanic uberhero understood what had been said, and answered, "Likewise. What are you?"

"In my land, I am called *oni.*"

There was no translation for this term, but the Blazing Scarab understood it. He said, "I have fought demons before."

"And I have fought mystics before ... and yet here I *stand*," retorted the Claw.

The Hispanic uberhero's scarab shot forth a bright beam of fire at the demonic being. A claw-like hand whipped up and caught the flames.

The Blazing Scarab found the walls suddenly closing in on him, and used the power of his amulet to keep them at bay. When his gaze returned to the Claw, he found the *oni* was growing.

The Scarab's mystical sense warned him that something was amiss. The uberhero sent a another flash of fire at the gigantic figure, causing its kimono to burst into flames. But the walls and ceiling had stopped moving, revealing this to be an illusion.

The Claw grinned, showing yellowed fang-like teeth. "You are mighty, Blazing Scarab. But it is inevitable that I shall prevail."

"You will try," gritted the Scarab.

## Chapter 17

## STORM WARNING

The grouping of Dr. Nemesis, Cerebex, Magno, and the Fighting Yank finally arrived at the location of the final samurai, the surrounding area having been more or less leveled by this time for a half mile in every direction. An entire neighborhood had vanished, leaving only rubble in its place.

Though it was a horrifying sight, the demeanor of the arriving uberheroes was one of fatigue. The creatures were not easy to defeat, even if the strategy was sound. Nemesis gave voice to their feelings: "I'm glad this is the last one."

"*I* hope the Scarab is having as much success as we are," offered Magno. Each knew what he meant: The creator of the infernal machines would be at least as dangerous as his creations, and among the full membership of the Guild, only the Scarab had any knowledge of magic.

On seeing the newcomers, the ebony samurai reacted as had its supernatural siblings: It ignored them until they made a threat of themselves. The battle went much as had the earlier ones: Magno contained it by manipulating the Earth's magnetic field with his staff, and caused ripples to form upon its shiny surface, weakening it. The Fighting Yank used his powerful CP beam on a bulge of metal. When it sought to escape the punishment, Dr. Nemesis and

Cerebex moved in to trap it.

Finally, an explosion of light burst from a small rent in the armor, releasing the spirit powering it. Then it collapsed, striking the broken ground with clankings.

Cerebex confessed, "I'm glad that's over."

As the Fighting Yank returned to his colleagues, Magno levitated the inanimate armor, and, flew it out over the Atlantic to drop it to join the others.

The Yank noticed the hairs on Dr. Nemesis' forearms standing on end.

"Static electricity," Nemesis volunteered. He sniffed the air. He was the only one of the three to be getting actual night air, the Fighting Yank's intake being filtered and Cerebex needing none at all. "A storm is coming .... None is expected, by the way."

Before any could speak, the living titan announced, "The light – !"

Neither Cerebex nor the Fighting Yank noticed the sudden absence of starlight, for there was a new moon, and not much illumination coming down from above. What was there was obscured because the Manhattan night sky was always brightly lit by artificial light.

As one, the trio of uberheroes turned. Behind them stood a giant creature that looked as if it had stepped out of a nightmare, with large fangs and even larger ears, garbed in a black kimono.

The Claw said, "Welcome to Hell."


Laughter boomed from above the three uberheroes as the Claw pointed his long fingernails at them. Lightning flew from their sharp tips, and struck each of the trio, causing them to writhe in pain. The voltage even overcame the insulation of the two armored heroes, though it did not short circuit them as one might expect.

Dr. Nemesis fell to the ground, wounded as the bright tendrils dissipated. Through gritted teeth, he said, "That's as much punishment as I've ever endured. Nice to know it didn't kill me."

The Fighting Yank and Cerebex launched themselves into the air, each directed at a giant hand. These closed around an uberhero and *squeezed*.

The green giant braced his armored body against the pressure, and sent electric current out through his fingertips. This had no effect upon the gigantic demon, who was grinning, exposing yellow fanglike teeth.

The Fighting Yank switched on his magnetic force shield, which kept the crushing fingers at bay. Staley's mind raced for a method to escape. While the shield was in use, he was prevented from using his ultra-hot charged particle beam.

Below, Dr. Nemesis hurried to the giant figure, and, grasping the hem of the magnificent kimono, began to *climb*. When he reached the knee, he attracted the attention of the Claw, who wiggled a leg, throwing the living titan off with sudden unexpected force. The demon then dropped his two captives, and began to gesticulate towards the dark sky above.

As the trio re-grouped, it began to rain. But this was no ordinary rain. It pelted the uberheroes, who found it thick, like molasses. And like molasses, it was sticky. They soon found they could not move, trapped like flies on fly paper.

With a satisfied smile, the Claw peered down at his trapped enemies. He scooped the trio up once it was obvious that they could no longer move. Holding them up to his face, cupped in both hands, he whispered to the semi-conscious humans, "And now, my little chicks, we shall join your mystical comrade."

## Chapter 18

## FAERIE TALE

The captive members of the Guild, who now floated above the floor in the penthouse of the Claw, enveloped in an invisible mystical field, writhed in pain. The demon had informed them he was softening up their souls for later use, like tenderizing meat.

Once more ensconced in his luxuriously-appointed abode, the Claw had resumed his guise of an aged Asian, feeble and helpless. His Yakuza henchmen seemed not to notice judging by the oblivious expressions on their flat faces, though their eyes appeared alert.

"Of all of you mortals," the ancient being said, "only you, Blazing Scarab, will appreciate my story.

"I am the last of my kind. A thousand years ago, we *oni* ran free in Nippon, pleasuring ourselves by terrorizing and torturing humans. None who lived could challenge us. An occasional samurai attempted to, but we prevailed. Then the Buddhist monks came, and, one by one, hunted us. Working together in a way that we *oni* did not, they captured and imprisoned us around the countryside."

The Claw cackled with glee. "You see, even *they* could not kill us. They lacked the will, possessing a naïve reverence for all life, even ours. But we are not immortal. The samurai had learned that if our flesh was pierced, we could be killed. Otherwise, we were invulnerable to harm, unless it was of a magical nature, and none possessed such knowledge in those days. You somehow discovered that is how my *own* samurai function."

Returning his gaze to the Blazing Scarab, he said, "But Buddhists do not kill. That was their fatal flaw. While the samurai uncovered the resting places of my brethren, slaughtering them, the zealots who captured me put me into a deep sleep and buried me under Mount Hiei, where I would have slumbered forever had I not been awakened by foolish humans last year.

"I *know* you sensed this, and so I shielded my whereabouts upon sensing *you*. That is how I eluded you until I was ready to strike."

"In the end ... you will be defeated," predicted the Blazing Scarab, his jaw clenched in pain.

The demon cackled at the proclamation. "Oh? Did I not *defeat* you? Did you *let* yourself be captured?"

"I have *foreseen* it."

Angrily, the Claw stepped forward, toward the Hispanic mystic. Gazing at the scarab upon his chest, he said, "Your amulet intrigues me. There is nothing like it in Nippon."

Placing his hand through the mystic barrier, the image distorted as if the appendage had entered water, the Claw's bony fingers reached toward the scarab. But as soon as his long, sharp fingernails danced across its rugged surface, the stone tile flashed bright light, and the appendage recoiled as if it had touched flames.

"There is a reason," the uberhero spat, "why I am called ... Blazing Scarab."

"How did you *do* that?" the Claw queried, his slanted red eyes narrowing. "Your power is nullified in my prison."

"The *scarab* ... did it. I ... am the *chosen one*," the Blazing Scarab gritted through clenched teeth. "You will never unlock ... the scarab's secrets .... They belong only to *me*."

"Perhaps it will give up its secrets after you *die*," the Claw suggested with a thin smile.

His face tight, the Blazing Scarab returned the smile. "How little you comprehend."

"Feh!" spat the Claw.

His captive writhed anew as the *oni* increased the level of pain each prisoner felt. Of them, only Dr. Nemesis showed little discomfort. Through clenched teeth, he spat, "We're not done yet."

Grinning, the Claw said, "Oh? I have defeated the most powerful of your 'Guild'. Who is there to rescue *you?*"

As if on cue, the remaining members of the Guild broke into the penthouse. Magno, his staff held out before him, led the group as he glided through the air. The Crusader, Jinx with him, was close behind. The Flame was in the air as well, propelled by rocket-like bursts from his hands. Kitten, Black Fury, and Dynamic Man followed in their own ways.

The Flame flew forward toward the Claw. The demon focused his attention on the fiery uberhero. The two grappled, the Claw seemingly immune to the Flame's blaze.

The Flame found the Claw's fingernails razor sharp. These sliced at his flesh. Stepping back, he increased the intensity of his flames. The Claw's kimono suddenly caught fire in a bright flash of flame.

Dynamic Man, with his uberhuman physique, was the first to reach the armed Yakuza gunmen the Claw employed. They had reacted instantly, hands pulling large black automatics from beneath their dark suit jackets. He bounded toward them with superhuman speed and agility, dodging most of the bullets that came his way. His yellow and scarlet costume made him the easy target, as both women were garbed in darker hues.

Dynamic Man's costume was not only bright. The yellow suit consisted of a fine mesh that resisted small caliber fire and deflected anything except a head-on slug of a larger size, while the scarlet breastplate was bulletproof. He would be bruised but uninjured the next day if he survived the next few minutes – and his superhuman healing factor would take care of those.

Leaping high into the air, the young uberhero came down at two of the gunmen, legs splayed. Each scarlet-booted foot struck one man in the face, knocking him out.

More thugs poured into the room. The Crusader led his squad into battle.

Across the enormous room, Magno floated before his imprisoned teammates. He held his staff before them, and, slowly, extracted the Fighting Yank and Cerebex from the field with sucking sound that ended in a loud, wet *snap*. It sounded more like *shnop*.

"How did you find us?" the green giant asked as the Fighting Yank entered the fray, going to the Flame's aid.

"I followed your armor," explained Magno in a modest tone. "My staff recognizes them as my eyes recognize them by sight. They have distinct qualities that make them unique. Excuse me, now I have two *more* to free."

"Right. And I'm needed elsewhere," Cerebex's electronic voice buzzed as he departed to join the battle.

Turning his attention to Dr. Nemesis and the

Blazing Scarab, the young Asian told them, "This may take some time. Neither of you have much metal on your person."

"Don't worry about me," Nemesis bellowed. "Get the Scarab out first. We're going to need him to beat the Claw.

"I can stand the pain."

"Ah, so, Doctor," returned Magno in an embarrassed tone. He was well aware of the living titan's uberpowers, having seen them in action many times since the pair – along with the Crusader and the Flame – had formed the Guild. He focused his staff on the Blazing Scarab, and slowly drew him from the mystical field. This took some time because the mystic had little metal on his person by which the staff could extract him. By the time he was free, the Flame was on the floor, unmoving, and by all appearances, the Fighting Yank, who had also attacked the Claw, was on his last legs.

Dr. Nemesis reiterated to Magno, "Leave me. You can end that gun battle in a few seconds."

Reluctantly, the young Japanese uberhero agreed, "Of course."

True to the living titan's prediction, the Claw's thugs were quickly disarmed by Magno's staff – their weapons suddenly yanked from their grasps. Those that still resisted were quickly rounded up and captured by the Crusader's squad.

The Blazing Scarab arrived just in time to prevent the demon, now virtually naked, his kimono having been burned away by the Flame's fire, from landing a killing blow to the Fighting Yank. The two faced one another again.

## Chapter 19

## SHOWDOWN

As the Claw flung lightning bolts at his foe, the sacred scarab of the mystic uberhero flashed, repelling them. They flew every which way, sizzling angrily as they dissipated.

With an animalistic growl, the demon flung himself forward, his claw-like nails scraped across Blazing Scarab's own force shield, but did not penetrate it. The mystic threw himself forward, taking the Claw's hands in his own. He said: "I did not allow you to capture me. Your magic was unfamiliar to me. But while I was your prisoner, I *studied* you. And I foresaw *how* I would defeat you."

When the Claw realized his strength was useless, he freed his hands from the Scarab's grasp, and pushed him away. A flame blazed from the scarab, following his path as he retreated. An expensive Middle Eastern rug caught fire. This quickly spread throughout the largest chamber of the penthouse.

The *oni* summoned dark clouds that appeared near the high ceiling of the chamber. But before they could gush their thick paralyzing rain down upon his enemies, the Blazing Scarab dispelled them with a bright burst of light from the tile on his ornamental breastplate.

While the mystic's attention was diverted, the Claw grew, and, reaching down, raked him with giant nails sharp as razors. The wounds drew a cry of pain from the Blazing Scarab.

Surrounding himself with a mystic force shield, he launched himself up at the Claw, and wrestled him to the floor with superhuman strength. Wrestling was a sport of the Olmecs, which the Blazing Scarab had learned during his century-long mystical slumber. One of the famous statues of that culture was of that profession, more than 2500 years old.

The two grappled. Their might seemed well matched, but the Japanese creature had no knowledge of hand-to-hand combat. Being so much more powerful than humans, he'd had no need to learn.

Once the mystic had the *oni* in the desired hold, he drew out his blade made of obsidian, sharp as the finest modern scalpel. Poising it above the Claw's chest, he said, "You never should have told me how to kill you."

With that, he plunged the dagger into the Claw's chest, and, scribing a circle in the sallow flesh, reached in and pulled out the demon's beating heart.

Mid scream, the Claw's body began to wither like a wilting flower, until all that remained were parchment-like ashes.


As the members of the Guild rounded up the captured Yakuza men, Dr. Nemesis, released from his mystic prison, joined Blazing Scarab, who informed him, "The Claw was very close to conquering the world."

"How so?"

"He hinted at it when he told us he was preparing our souls for future use. He was using the souls of those killed in the rampages of the four samurai to fuel future unholy creatures. These would increase in number geometrically, the dead of one city providing him with enough souls to conquer a hundred more. If we had not stopped him here, we might never have done so."

"I imagine he came here to New York to test his samurai against us, and if he defeated us, no one would be left to stop him," remarked Nemesis.

"Possibly," the Blazing Scarab mused. "But New York City is considered the capital of the world, and perhaps he hoped to inspire terror in everyone in the world all at once. The *oni* lived to terrorize humans, remember."

"A good strategy," agreed the living titan. As the Blazing Scarab began to rise into the air, Nemesis asked him, "Where are you going?"

Holding the demon's heart up, the mystic explained, "To properly dispose of this in an ancient ritual."

Flying through one of the windows that had been shattered during the battle, he headed south, pointing himself toward his hidden temple.

## THE END

Afterword

## THE PLOT BEHIND THE CURTAIN, OR, A WALK THROUGH THE PLOT

I wrote this to aid a friend in plotting a story, a step-by-step guide to how I developed this plot. I do this with every book, though I don't organize my random thoughts in such a detailed manner as I generate plot points until I have enough to write the actual plot, when I begin to see a chain of events developing. This normally entails *pages* of notes as ideas are jotted down and either incorporated into a developing plot or discarded. There are always false starts and dead ends, some of which can be recycled into later stories.

But to be honest, I don't think this is the best example of how to plot, generally, because I used my own version of Lester Dent's famous 4-part outline, which he used to write his short stories (but *not*, contrary to Jim Steranko's claim in *The Steranko History of Comics*, to write Doc Savage novels; the "master outline" was stated by Dent to be designed for short stories of about 6000 words, which is why I expanded it to six parts to write novels).

So this plot didn't evolve in a way that I'd call "naturally", *organically*. It's "artificial", for lack of a better word, because it uses a master outline. One of the other things I wanted to try with this story in addition to those mentioned in the Foreword was to plot it as a pulp story, rather than as a comic book story as I normally do. You will note that the finished story deviates in a few places from this plot, as I incorporate new ideas as I write.

To begin with – even before I knew who the *heroes* were going to be – I chose the Claw as the main antagonist because he's the most famous public domain supervillain, really the only *high-level* "master" villain I could think of off the top of my head. Not that there aren't others who *could* be in his league, but none are so well known as he. He has sort of an Asian look to him, IMO, which started me researching Asian mythology. I discarded a *lot* of stuff about dragons, *pages* of information, which was my first idea: dragons of the natural elements, which, according to the Chinese philosophy *wuxing* are: fire, wood, air, earth, and metal. I may yet use this material somewhere.

One of the things I thought about the Claw was he vaguely resembled those frightful Japanese masks of demons. I was familiar with the *oni*, a special type of demon who began life as a mortal who refused to pass over to the other side; some were men so evil they refused to even *die*. So he is an *oni* in this UH&BH universe, and more resembles the aforementioned masks than he does the comic book Claw.

Since Japan is known for equal parts mythology/mysticism and technology, the idea that the Claw is using technology to make magic came to me, since the *oni* apparently couldn't cast spells.

It took me a day or two to figure this out after I'd done my demon research. Then I recalled one of the HELLRAISER films where the descendant of the original box maker builds a space station to trap Pinhead. I kept thinking, and reversed that premise:

The Claw is not using technology to make magic, but magic to make technology. So the idea of animated samurai armor came to me. This is an evocative image, and it fits with the era the Claw originally lived in.

But how does the armor work? I recalled that *oni* are cannibals so the Claw is *eating* humans, and trapping their *souls* in the armor! They are unstoppable by normal human means. They *must* be, in odrer to give our heroes a hard time.

But what is the Claw's goal? Or motive? Plots for pulp stories revolve around what the bad guy is doing – and he has to have a motive, a goal, and a plan to accomplish his goal. *Oni* are pure evil and occupy their time terrorizing humans. That's it. So *that*, I decided, would be the entire story: His "samurai" are causing terror in the streets of New York. For fun.

*But* ... with every human that his samurai kill, he is able to trap its soul for use in another suit of armor. This is his goal, and his plan is to amass an army that will take over the world. This turns him from a mass sadist to a global threat.

With this return of the spirits of the dead, this is will likely take place over less than 24 hours on November 1 – "Day of the Dead", when the spirits of the dead return to a semblance of life, I decided.

Beginnings of stories are easiest for me, and right away, I had the image of an archaeologist finding a well-preserved corpse. As the expedition studies the corpse, its eyes open. End of scene. I filled this out with some background to set the time and place – important to establish early in any story (especially in the case of *fictional* worlds), and build suspense.

I had an idea that the last of these Chapter 1 scenes would be the Claw in New York City, in a new guise – but decided this left too big a gap in the story.

What happens in the story in the two chapters before his attack in Chapter 4 (the first real battle according to Dent's outline)? So the Claw's introduction in the present is better off in either CH 3 or CH 4.

Which brings us to what I call "the rough plot", the plot points which are organized into a sequence. This is the backbone of the story that the outline is built upon. I outline everything I write. The longer the story, the more detailed the outline.

This is a very simple plot, the simplest I've ever tried for a novel, because it takes place over such a short period of time – less than eight hours probably – and involves a single event: the battle for Manhattan. This also creates a lot of restrictions, though, when it comes to plotting. It is not a mystery with clues to find and leads to follow.

The plot points are: The bad guy is introduced; the heroes are introduced; the bad guy's plan begins with an attack; the heroes respond; they are repelled and re-group; repeat; they find a way to win; they do so but there's a snag; the big wrap-up. How exactly this unfolds will be determined by Dent's master 4-part plot, which I use in *every* pulp novel I write.

Dent's outline has a fight in every section (I make each "section" a chapter, generally), so I decided that these would be the first to establish. This is especially applicable with this story being a straightforward novel-length fight.

CH 4   Introduction of samurai. Though 4 of them are released all at once (4 is an unlucky number in both Japanese and Chinese because it sounds like the word for "death"), *one* must arrive at its destination first. So that one is introduced in CH 4. Cops arrive and are quickly defeated.

CH 7   One of the heroes stumbles on a samurai and is also repelled.

CH 11  Responding to the threat, the members of the Guild fight the 4 samurai (which is what the armor looks like). After being defeated and having to retreat (in CH 7), one hero points out that fighting them solo is impossible – they'll never win. They have to work in groups to defeat the samurai.

CH 15  This tactic works. We jump from fight to fight to see that it's working.

CH 19  The final samurai is defeated. Then the Claw makes an appearance, beginning the climax of the story.

The next step, when working with Dent's outline in this way, is to then fill in the blanks according to the descriptions of the sections of the outline (such as "bury the hero in troubles", "the hero struggles", "fight", etc.). This paces the story and varies the events, such as mixing up the mode of combat, guns, fists, knives, whatever, from section to section.

I don't always plot a Dent-outline story starting with the fights, but sometimes do, if I'm having trouble plotting. Different methods of plotting work for different stories. I can't really explain why, or how I know which method to use when. There's a groove to some stories that comes naturally. Other times, it's work to plot a story. But usually, with my adapted Dent outline, I can plot a novel in 1-3 days. If it takes longer, it's not because of the story as much as real life distractions that make it so that I can't focus on writing. The shortest time I've plotted a novel was under an hour, and have only done that *twice* in a hundred novel outlines.

The in-between chapters can help lead into a fight, or deal with the aftermath of one – a process I use for *all* plotting. This can give you good scenes that you might not otherwise think of in plotting a story. Sometimes I have ideas for scenes around the fights, either something leading into the fight or coming out of it – and though this isn't necessary per the outline, that's usually the easiest way to plot it. I had no ideas of this sort here, so I started at the beginning.

Since the "Hero" of Chapter 1 is killed therein, I needed a new "Hero" for Chapter 2. The only mystic hero I have is the Blazing Scarab, so he's it. It is obvious that since he is a mystic, he senses the Claw's resurrection. He tries to locate him but his target simply disappears (the Claw reacting to the mystic probe he senses). In order to keep Blazing Scarab away from NYC (since that's where the Claw will strike), I thought he could have had a dream about the Claw, and awakened – a premonition.

One thing different I'm doing in this superhero story from the other first volumes of superhero series I've written (I have nine or ten of these superhero universes in print – I just have too many incompatible ideas to use everything in a single milieu) is that not every superhero will get his or her origin told. I've done this in a few books – inspired by Alan Moore's WATCHMEN – and I wanted to do it differently here, only tell origins that related naturally to the events of the story. These are not necessarily the origins of my favorite characters. If there are other novels to follow, eventually I'd work in the origins of all eleven main characters (and future members).

So the Blazing Scarab's origin is told in CH 2 because it relates to the action therein. I think this information is important to the story, so readers know what the Blazing Scarab can do – and why, without a lot of expository dialogue ("Say, it's lucky you've fought demons before, BS!"). BS indeed.

In the master outline, Chapter 3 introduces all the other major characters, i.e., the "uberheroes". Since there was no obvious way to me to introduce them in any meaningful way in relation to the attack in Chapter 4 since it's a *surprise* attack, I decided the Blazing Scarab calls an emergency meeting in 2023 to warn everyone of the resurrected evil. But since this would be a possibly boring and probably short chapter, I chose to write a vignette for each character as he or she receives the emergency alert, to introduce them. I avoided the superhero convention of revealing everything about a character upon introduction – or tried to. So readers have to connect some dots in these vignettes, a result of the hard $3^{RD}$ POV.

After the initial attack in Chapter 4, the heroes must respond – it is now over a year after the Blazing Scarab's warning, and he must reveal this is the menace he's sensed earlier – even though the source is diffuse and vague (so he can't locate it and thus cut short the story). Chapters 5-7 all had to feature the same hero (or heroes), IMO – it doesn't make sense to me to introduce a character and continue his story in CH 6, then switch to another character in CH 7 (the second fight of the story, remember).

It took me three tries to get the right hero for this sequence. I settled on the Crusader because him fighting against an unbeatable foe would highlight his never-say-die attitude. It also works out then to squeeze in his origin, starting with the origin of his sidekick Jinx, due to *how* the pair is introduced here.

The events of CH 8-10 must lead from the previous fight to the next – particularly because the events of the entire story take place over a single night, and describe a single battle – so I thought about the aftermath of the earlier fight and what must precede the next for a logical plot. I often have found it useful in pulp stories to figure out the why and who of the fights (after plotting the first 4 or so chapters, the easiest part of every story I've ever written) and then fill in the blanks. *While trying not to be predictable*, a danger in using a "master outline".

In this case, the hero retreats to HQ where he informs his teammates what he knows. They decide on a plan of action while the military takes over – what *else* could happen while our heroes are busy elsewhere? They can't sit around just talking between fights. So others have to take the lead spot once in a while, or subplots introduced. *Everything* must be *logical*, and if it can't be that, it must be *reasonable*. And if you can't make it either of these, you'd better have a damned good explanation for something illogical and unreasonable to happen. Weak plots are a pet peeve of mine. Here, the Crusader, the current leader of the Guild, splits the team into pairs, one for each robot, with Blazing Scarab busy trying to find the vague source behind the attacks.

The progressions of the fights, I've determined since this is one long battle, is that here (CH 11), the heroes all lose, fighting what looks like an unbeatable foe (jumping from fight to fight so readers get a good idea of who each hero is and what they can do). In the next fight (CH 15), they defeat one of the samurai, which then leads to them being able to defeat the final three in CH 19. This is a logical string of events and a good enough backbone for the plot for me.

The "surprise" here (CH 12) doesn't have to be big as much as it has to be important. Usually, I just settle for any surprise I can throw the readers' way. The first surprise here is that a downed/defeated robot recovers, ala the Terminator, leading to speculation how this is possible. It works out here that the bigger surprise is the Blazing Scarab discovers that magic is involved – the "robots" are not "mere machines": The mystical menace has fused magic and machine. I'd originally considered the *big reveal* here but decided to save that for later. It's so big it feels like it should be shown in the climax of the story. This also fits with the defeat of one of the "samurai" robots in Chapter 15.

So the four samurai now seem impossible to beat – the Blazing Scarab *cannot* be able to defeat one by himself, or else the story would end quickly. He'd just "zap" each one, and bang (or rather, whimper), the story would essentially be over.

But it may turn out he will need to be able to affect them in some way without actually defeating them single-handedly. He might have to figure out what his teammates have to do to beat them, or aid them in some other way.

The team decides to marshal all their forces against a single samurai, and, in Chapter 15, they do defeat it – by cracking the armor open. This breaks the enchantment; this goes back to my Japanese research, where an *oni* could be cut with a samurai sword and thereby be defeated/killed. The Blazing Scarab says this makes sense, belatedly. The big surprise for Chapter 16 is that the armor is *empty*. This leads the Blazing Scarab to deduce that the machines are powered by trapped souls (*the BIG reveal*), though he doesn't announce this as perhaps the realization comes to him slowly. There's a lot going on to occupy his mind at the moment.

After showing the Claw and his reaction to one of his samurai being defeated (which feels like a necessity), Chapters 17-18 is more running around & strategizing, and involves calling off conventional tactics which have been escalating. Again, what else could be going on in the background? The president is considering using a weapon that will destroy some of the city to stop the samurai, a last resort weapon. Dramatically, the un-powered (AKA *weaker*) heroes intervene just in time to stop massive destruction and loss of life.

The reason to split the team here is to ratchet up the tension and suspense – if the stronger heroes fail, what chance to do the weaker heroes have? This sets up the climax.

Now knowing all they have to do is *penetrate* the samurai armor to stop it, the remainder of the Guild – the stronger heroes – go to fight another samurai, and beat it. In quick succession, they stop the final two after this. It may be that it's at this time that the Blazing Scarab realizes that souls are powering the armor – now that he's seen/felt it done four times.

You will note that not all details are nailed down as I work out the rough plot on the way to the finished plot, and then the outline. Even some details in the outline are changed as I write the story. There are some things in every story I write that I don't know is going to be there until I write them – no matter how detailed my outlines. That is part of the magic of writing.

But this isn't the end: There are a few more chapters to go, but the fight in Chapter 19 begins the climax traditionally (although I *have* experimented in starting it earlier (as early as Chapter 13) and putting it off a chapter or two, simply for variety's sake). The Claw shows up (dramatically at the end of CH 19 while the team is celebrating), and (in CH 20) attacks the team with magic. This is powerful enough to defeat them, but it's not devastation on a wide scale, which is why he used the samurai for that. Again: Explain why things happen the way they do. Don't leave loose ends lying around at the end of your story.

Things look bad for the powerhouses of the team as they are captives of the Claw, who reveals his origin here as an *oni*, how he was defeated by the Buddhist monks a thousand years ago and imprisoned beneath the temple on Mt. Hiei where he was found and awakened, etc., while magically torturing his captives before killing them – just for fun. He's also intrigued by "beta humans" (superhumans) but this is secondary – he can learn about them by studying their souls after they're dead. This is for readers who missed these ideas early in the book. Unless you're trying to write an ambiguous ending, readers should have no questions at the end of your story. This is one of the flaws of beginning writers: They forget that readers don't know everything *they* know about the characters.

The Claw believed his samurai to be invincible, and once the members of the Guild are dead, they will be again. Things look grim for the captive heroes when the weaker team members, led by the Crusader, arrive to rescue the stronger ones. The Blazing Scarab leads the attack on the Claw, keeping him busy while the weaker heroes fight the henchmen (probably Japanese Yakuza whom he's enthralled) and free the stronger heroes. The Blazing Scarab may or may not be strong enough to defeat the Claw on his own.

Chapters 23-24 in the outline will be combined, since they would be short chapters revealing the final secrets of the Claw, clearing up all the mysteries: The Blazing Scarab has figured out his plan having mystically inspected the samurai, and reveals the geometric building of the Claw's spirit army: He captured the souls of the people his samurai kill, to be used in *new* samurai suits. Which would then move on to a nearby city to repeat the process, until the entire Earth had been conquered.

The epilogue is, while the heroes celebrate at Guild House, the Blazing Scarab takes the unconscious Claw (who is immortal in keeping with the origin of the *oni* being so evil they refuse to die) to his hidden temple in Mexico, where he's sealed in a room that is mystically hidden and protected so no one will ever awaken him again.

## APPENDIX OF SOURCE CHARACTERS

Note that these characters have no connection to those used in this book except as providing a name.

PROTAGONISTS
Black Fury (Fox)
The Blazing Scarab (Worth Carnahan/Harvey)
Cerebex (Fiction House)
The Crusader (Hillman)
Douglas Drew, Ghost-Breaker (ACG)
Dr. Nemesis (Ace)
Dynamic Man (Chesler)
The Fighting Yank (Nedor)
The Flame (Fox)
Jinx (Lev Gleason)
Kitten (Holyoke)
Magno (Ace)

ANTAGONISTS
The Black Axeman (Fiction House)
Blitz (Fox)
The Claw (Lev Gleason)
Dr. Death II (Fawcett)
Dr. Fission (Nedor)
The Shinto Samurai (Ace)

Jeff Deischer is best known for his chronologically-minded essays, particularly the book-length *The Man of Bronze: a Definitive Chronology*, about the pulp DOC SAVAGE series. It is *a* definitive chronology, rather than *the* definitive chronology, he explains, because each chronologist of the DOC SAVAGE series has his own rules for constructing his own chronology. Jeff believes his own chronology to be the definitive one – using his rules, which were set down by Philip Jose Farmer in his book, *Doc Savage: His Apocalyptic Life*.

Jeff was born in 1961, a few years too late, in his opinion. He missed out on the Beatles, the beginning of the Marvel Age of comic books and the early years of the Bantam reprints of the DOC SAVAGE series, the latter two of which he began reading when he was about ten years old (on the other hand, he was too young to go to Viet Nam ….).

Jeff had become enamored of Heroes – with a capital "H", for these were not *ordinary* men – at a very young age. He grew up watching DANIEL BOONE (to whom he is distantly related, by marriage), TARZAN, BATMAN, THE LONE RANGER and ZORRO on television. There is a large "Z" carved into his mother's sewing machine that can attest to this fact (as you might imagine, it did not impress her the way it always did the peasants and soldiers on ZORRO).

This genre of fiction made a lasting impression on his creative view, and everything he writes has Good Guys and Bad Guys – in capital letters. As an adult writer, he tries to make his characters *human*, as well.

Jeff began writing as a young teenager, and, predictably, all of it was bad. He started to write seriously while in college, but spent the next decade creating characters and universes and planning stories without seeing much of it to fruition. This wasted time is his biggest regret in life.

In the early 1990s, Jeff began a correspondence with noted pulp historian and novelist Will Murray, while he was writing both the DOC SAVAGE and THE DESTROYER series (THE DESTROYER #102 is actually dedicated to Jeff). Jeff currently consults on Will Murray's DOC SAVAGE books (as evidenced by the acknowledgements pages in the novels of "The Wild Adventures of ..." series), a privilege that he enjoys. Will Murray's sage advice helped turn Jeff into a true author.

Producing few books over the next few years, Jeff's writing finally attained professional grade, and, after being laid off from the auto industry in 2007, he was able to devote more time to writing. From 2008, he produced an average of three books a year, most of it fiction, and most of that pulp. Reading so much of the writing of Lester Dent, the first, most prolific and best of those using the DOC SAVAGE house name "Kenneth Robeson", Jeff's own natural style is similar to Dent's. He "turns this up" when writing pulp, and "turns this down" when writing non-pulp fiction.

Jeff primarily writes fiction, and, combining his twin loves of superheroes and pulp, began THE GOLDEN AGE series in 2012. This resurrected, revamped and revitalized the largely forgotten characters of Ned Pines' Standard, Better and Nedor publishing companies. These characters, drawn from superhero, pulp and mystic milieus, fill the "Auric Universe", as Jeff calls it.

Jeff's webpage is jeffdeischer.blogspot.com, where he posts the first chapters of his novels, so that potential readers can peruse his work without having to spend several dollars on a trade paperback to find out if they like it or not.

# The Westerntainment Library

**Non-Fiction**

*Over the Rainbow: a User's Guide to My Dangyang* by Jeff Deischer
Dangyang – the real China. This is not the China you've seen in movies or on television – ramshackle villages or burgeoning metropolises indistinguishable from those of the West, but a small city unseen by Western tourists – an example of the real China. With over 40 pages of photos, you will come to know – and perhaps appreciate – Dangyang via a firsthand look at its customs, architecture and everyday ways -- through the eyes of the only American ever to visit it! Written informally, this is an expanded version of my journals on several trips to China.

*The Marvel Timeline Project, Part 1* by Jeff Deischer and Murray Ward
The Marvel Timeline Project is a chronology of Marvel Comics in the Silver Age written by expert chronologist and Marvel aficionado Jeff Deischer, and Marvel historian and official indexer Murray Ward. It includes *all* the comic series published at the time. Part 1 covers the first four years of the "Marvel Age" (from about 1961-64) and includes synopses of every story.

*The Way They Were: the Histories of Some of Adventure Fiction's Most Famous Heroes and Villains* by Jeff Deischer
Have you ever wondered when Victor Frankenstein created his monster? Or when

Dracula terrorized England? How about Captain Nemo's past? *The Way They Were* takes an in-depth look at the life and times of some of adventure fiction's most famous heroes and most notorious villains from the 1840s through the 1950s. Inside you'll find not only the answers to the above questions, but those to many more, covering characters as diverse as Korak, Son of Tarzan, James Bond, and the Phantom of the Opera – who, it is revealed, is related to none other than Doc Savage and Sam Spade of Maltese Falcon fame! The final section is a combined chronology of this "Shared Fictional Universe".

*Volume 1: The Victorian Age*
*Volume 2: The Pulp Era*
*Volume 3: Action Heroes*

*The Adventures of the Man of Bronze: a Definitive Chronology* (3$^{rd}$ ed.) by Jeff Deischer
The landmark chronology of Doc Savage, which first discovered the Man of Bronze's true birthday and included the radio plays in a timeline, is back in print in an expanded and updated edition that has been fully revised for better readability and easier consulting. It addition to including Will Murray's new Wild Adventures of Doc Savage, a number of the author's groundbreaking essays on the Man of Bronze are also contained within, including some that have only seen limited publication. Offered here for the first time anywhere is an expanded family tree that shows Doc Savage's possible relationships to other literary characters such as Sam Spade (Maltese

Falcon), Wolf Larsen (Sea Wolf), the Phantom of the Opera and Frankenstein's Monster!

*Baker's Dozen* by Jeff Deischer
All of Jeff Deischer's Doc Savage essays collected in one volume, with two new ones plus an interview with Will Murray when he was finishing the last WILD ADVENTURES OF DOC SAVAGE. **KINDLE ONLY**

**Superhero Fiction**
OVERWORLD series by Kim Williamson (Jeff Deischer)
A look at constructing a superhero universe from scratch, without the building blocks of comic books. This starts with a few simple premises and builds from there.

*The Overman Paradigm* (#1)
A collection of short stories that introduce the "atomic age" heroes of Overworld.

THE GOLDEN AGE series by Jeff Deischer
Published from 1939-56, the Standard/Better/Nedor characters are largely forgotten by today's comic book fans. THE GOLDEN AGE series uses Ned Pines' characters to weave together a coherent universe.

*The Golden Age, Volume II: Mystico*
1940: The Nazis are obsessed with mystical artifacts. Believing one was hidden in America centuries ago by the mysterious Knights Templar, the black wizard Nacht sends a party led by the sorcerer the Baron to find it. Nacht is as much a mystery to the Nazi hierarchy as he is to the rest

of the world. Claiming to be one of the Earth's "secret masters", he helped Hitler climb to power after the failed 1923 beer hall *putsch*, tutoring him in occult ways. He is aided in his quest by Reinhard Heydrich, the infamous "Hangman", who now controls the dreaded *Vril* power, becoming Nietzsche's *Ubermensch*. In this exciting prequel to the groundbreaking *The Golden Age*, the Auric Universe's mystical heroes must join forces to stop Nazi Germany from gaining one of the greatest prizes of all!

*The Golden Age, Volume III: Dark of the Moon*
The Auric Universe's oddball, fringe and civilian heroes get play here as cities are being destroyed by mysterious tidal waves. Dr X, an "occult scientist" sends his team, which includes his niece Cynthia, her fiance Bob Stone, Judy of the Jungle and her companion Pistols Roberts of Europol, and a patchwork giant called Jobe, to investigate.

*The Golden Age, Volume IV: The Golden Age*
In 1942, the world is at war. Spies and saboteurs seem to lurk around every corner in America. But, in the shadows, real danger awaits. Following the Battle of Midway, the Dragon Society of Imperial Japan sends agents on a secret mission to knock the U.S. out of the war. And only the superheroes of the Auric Universe can stop them.

*The Golden Age, Volume X: Future Tense*
Like many other heroes of the Auric Universe, Major Future seemed to come from nowhere. In his case, it was more true than in others'. In 1943,

a man with superhuman powers that included strength, agility and the ability to see radio waves, found himself in Los Angeles. How he got there and why he had these special abilities, he did not know. Impelled by some inner drive to help others, he took the name "Major Future" and became a superhero. *Future Tense* tells the full origin of the hero known as Major Future.

*The Golden Age, Volume XI: Bad Moon Rising*
The spotlight is on Major Wonder, an homage to the fun (i.e., smartass) superheroes of the Silver Age. In this volume containing six independent but interrelated novelettes adapted from his series in MYSTERY and WONDER, he faces dark times that run the gamut from superhero to horror to Sci-Fi.

In THE STEEL RING series, R. A. Jones returns to the Centaur characters in a new, pulpier iteration than his Malibu Comics series THE PROTECTORS.

*The Steel Ring*
The Centaur characters join forces during World War II as the Steel Ring.

*The Twilight War*
Members of the Steel Ring go overseas to battle the enemy.

*The House of Souls*
The members of the Steel Ring split up to deal with two threats, and make a stand at Pearl Harbor.

*A Ring of Worlds*
Flung through space and time, the members of the Steel Ring desperately try to return to their home.

The ARGENT series by Jeff Deischer
The Argentverse is an homage to the Silver Age of comic books, with the sensibilities of the Seventies.

*Argent*
This volume contains three novellas, each featuring different characters over the summer of 1961: Vanguard, Jr., Miss Adventure, Kid Thunderbolt and Blitz, the children of the golden age mystery men "The Three Musketeers"; The Stargazer, an alien stranded on Earth; Shadowalker, a young Navajo man who learns of his mystic heritage.

*Night of the Owl*
1946: World War II is over and the world is changing. While the Axis has been defeated, a new menace threatens the globe: Communism. When industrialist Owen S. Grane is brutally murdered, the Three Musketeers, America's foremost superheroes, are called in to find the culprit, who attacks and kills like a wild animal. Was it the Soviets? A spurned lover? A cheated business rival? Or someone else? One by one, upper level executives of the S.M.A. Corporation, an American defense contractor, are attacked and killed in a savage manner, until, finally the Owl reveals himself – but only after a cat-and-mouse game with the Three Musketeers.

*The Superlatives*
In 1958, the Superlatives were formed: Professor Amos Abercrombie, archaeologist and believer in things occult; his fiery daughter Amy Abercrombie, who can do anything a man can do; feisty reporter Red McAllister, who is after that one big story; Don Farnsworth, big game hunter who has utter confidence in his skill with a gun. Together they roam the globe looking for adventure and mystery. In 1960, they discover something more remarkable than any of their previous expeditions, one that changes their lives forever. This takes them around half the world, where they meet the superheroes of the Soviet Union, Australia, Communist China and Japan before returning home to confront an old enemy.

*Strange Days*
Strange Days Indeed. The 1950s were a time of hidden menace in America. Communist spies lurked around every corner and the bomb could drop at any moment. No one was above suspicion. It is into these times that the Mysterians appear. The patients of the Destry Clinic are freaks, possessing superhuman abilities – but superhuman appearances as well. They cannot simply remove a costume and disappear into a crowd. They are unlike the other heroes of the Argentverse. Dr. Destiny, the mysterious, unseen leader of the Mysterians. Mach, whose ability to fly at tremendous speed is slowly killing him. NRG, who must wear cumbersome armor to protect others from his deadly energy. Metallica, who possesses metal skin. The Mysterians face equally astonishing menaces, including Gargantua, who can mold his form

into any shape; the Brain, a criminal mastermind with a superhuman mind; the stunning Sorcerer, who can perform seeming miracles; the Gauntlet and his Insidians.

*Modern Times*
Modern Times contains three novellas set in the future of the Argentverse -- our present (the early 2000s). These stories are daring, ambitious and experimental, pushing the boundaries of the author's works. Darkstorm and Morningstar are a married crimefighting couple. The Golden Ghost is a pulp hero set in the modern era. The Crusader is obsessed with stopping the madman whom he believes to be his partner and friend. WARNING: adult-ish content

*Mystery Men*
Mystery Men contains three interrelated short stories, as the Crimson Crusader (a vigilante), Karma (a martial artist) and Dr. Stellar (a scientist) each face a different aspect of a deadly threat to mankind. These heroes bridge the gap between pulp vigilantes and superheroes, operating in the 1936 Argentverse.

THE AGE OF AQUARIUS series by Jeff Deischer
This features Jack "King" Kirby's public domain characters of the 1940s and '50s, bringing them together for the first time.

*The Strange Harvest of Dr. Aquarius* (#1)
In 1976, America's Greatest Patriot is murdered! And while the nation's other superheroes attempt

to solve this heinous crime, a new race of superhumans emerges – *Homo Nova!*

THE HERITAGE UNIVERSE by Jeff Deischer
A small coherent public domain superhero universe centered on the Charlton charters.

*Hide and Seek* (201)
Familiar mystery men and women band together as the Sentinels to confront a mysterious menace that threatens the entire Earth.

*Tag, You Are It!* (202)
The Sentinels deal with various problems while a strange plague engulfs South America. This story resolves a long-standing dangling subplot from a Charlton story.

*Duck Duck Goose* (203)
The international criminal organization the W.E.B. was all but destroyed by U.N.I.O.N. – until a mysterious new leader gathered up the loose threads that remained, and re-built it – then directed it against the Sentinels.

*War!* (204)
The gods of old return – to wage war on one another as they did centuries past. And the Sentinels are caught in the middle when an old villain returns.

*New World Order* (1001)
Billionaires all over the world are disappearing, and U.N.I.O.N. agents (who work for the United Nations) are called into investigate. This is a

unique experimental story that is not your typical superheroes vs. supervillains.

*Peek-a-Boo* (2000)
Two generations of heroes battle a menace that will conquer the world in this time- and dimension-hopping adventure that spans the Silver Age of the Heritage Universe.

*Toy Soldiers* (200)
Finally, the secret origin of the sensational Sentinels! When an unusual menace threatens the earth, five mystery men (and woman) must band together to stop it!

*Inner Space* (101)
The agent of U.N.I.O.N. face a menace unlike they've faced before, and follow the trail back to a land more foreign than they can imagine.

*Split Decision* (102)
The agents of A.Q.U.A. face the combined threat of two old foes who return with an audacious plan to control the world's oceans.

*Hero U.N.I.O.N.: the Next Generations Parts 1 and 2* (103, 104)
Two volumes of short stories about the new heroes and heroines who take up the mantle of U.N.I.O.N. a decade after the original agents.

## THE NEW ROUND TABLE by Jeff Deischer

*2020 The New Round Table*
A new wave of superheroes emerge in San Francisco to deal with the mysterious object known as the Grail – and those who seek to unlock its secrets.

*The Sixth Men* by Jeff Deischer
The Holyoke characters are rebooted to the 21$^{st}$ century in a plot to take over the world that draws in characters old and new to stop it.

## HERO 8 UNIVERSE by Jeff Deischer
*1967 Summer of Hate*
Three new superheroes face the cult of the Stone Buddha in three short stories.
KINDLE ONLY

**Science Fiction**
BRAVE NEW WORLD series by Lawrence V. Bridgeport (Jeff Deischer)
Passengers of a luxury space liner are forced to abandon ship onto a wild, harsh world, where they organize into socio-political groups – while fighting for their survival.

*Divided We Planetfall* (#1)
The captain of the ship attempts to unite everyone into a common community. Some factions welcome the opportunity to join. Others don't.

THE BROTHERHOOD OF SABOURS series by Wes T. Salem (Jeff Deischer)

Psychic warrior-priests armed with weapons powered by mental energy, the Brotherhood of Sabours has been keeping peace in the galaxy for thousands of years. Now a new menace threatens that peace: the Sund. Mysterious and powerful, the Sund's secrets are difficult to uncover. Its members are unknown -- even the number of members is unknown, as is the organization's scheme, which includes the destruction of the Brotherhood and the Galactic Union.

*The Brotherhood of Sabours Book One: The Shadow of the Sund*

*The Brotherhood of Sabours Book Two: The Reavers of Kargh*

*The Brotherhood of Sabours Book Three: The Red Brotherhood*

*The Heart of the Universe*
A standalone novel set a generation after the Brotherhood of Terror, Sabour Rebani Kalba comes across what seems to be a sentient gem. Investigating this with the help of adventurer-archaeologist Bal Tabarin, the Sabour finds that there are a number of such gems, the gathering of which will lead to an undescribed but momentous event. The pair races to find the fragments of the gem even as others do the same.

WORLDS COLLIDE series by Jeff Deischer
A series of sequels to the famous science fiction novel, *When Worlds Collide*, and its sequel, *After Worlds Collide*.

*Beyond Worlds Collide* (#3)
The story begins a few months after *After Worlds Collide* ends, and picks up some of dangling plot threads and answers unanswered questions, such as, What happened to the Other People? *Beyond Worlds Collide* is faithful to the original two novels in style and tone, and true space opera: The themes of the series are grand ones, the destruction of Earth, the establishing of a new home for humans and contact with alien life.

*War of Worlds Collide* (#4)
A new menace arises on Bronson Beta to threaten the settlement of Earth's refugees. Someone – or some*thing* – has declared war on the humans!

*Under Worlds Collide* (#5)
An old menace returns to threaten Earth's colonies on Bronson Beta while the first murder in Hendron-Khorlu occurs.

SINNERS & SAINTS series by Jeff Deischer
In the 38th century, three convicts escape the prison planet Purgatory and find themselves in a lawless region of space known as the Borderlands.

*Four on the Run* (#1)
Escape is just the beginning of the convicts' adventures. Contains three novelettes, each of which is analogous to an hour-long TV episode.

*Four in the Way* (#2)
Continues the misadventures of the four criminals in three novelettes.

FARSPACE series by Jeff Deischer
An homage to Star Trek.

*The Gates of Heaven* (#1)
In the 24$^{th}$ century, the deep space cruiser *Natty Bumppo* discovers a planet where a powerful being resides – and claims to be God. A thoughtful, philosophical mystery.

*Three on a Match* by Jeff Deischer
Inspired by Spaghetti Western films, the story is set on Mars in a hundred years, made habitable due to terraforming. Along its equator sits the cities that comprise civilization. Beyond this lies Nu West, the frontier which in many ways resembles the Old West. Three disparate men each learn of a stolen treasure and clues to its whereabouts. None of them know all the details of where the treasure is supposed to be, so, at times, they are forced to work together. They face many dangers, both individually and together, in pursuit of their quest, including each other.

"Infection" by Jeff Deischer
The crew of a tramp freighter makes first contact with aliens when it finds a derelict military corsair, and the mystery of what really happened there. KINDLE ONLY

**Pulp Fiction**
ADVENTURERS, INC. series by Jeff Deischer
Back after more than sixty-five years, Adventurers, Inc. goes into action.

*Spook Trail* (#1)
Who or what is terrorizing the people of Weeping Hollow? The Scare Devil spook had been haunting Weeping Hollow for two hundred years – but when people started disappearing, Adventurers, Inc. was called in to find out why!

THE CHALLENGER series by Jeff Deischer
In the tradition of Doc Savage, the Avenger and the Shadow comes ... the Challenger. Wrongly convicted of a crime he did not commit, the man who would become the Challenger swore to help others who could not help themselves. Joined by a group of assistants – experts in their own endeavors – the Challenger rights wrongs sand punishes evil-doers.

*The Winter Wizard* (#1)
In August 1947, Challenger finds himself up against the weird menace of the Winter Wizard – a madman who is able to control the weather!

*The Little Book of Short Stories: 9 Weird Tales* by Jeff Deischer
Nine short stories in a variety of genres: Historical, pulp (a new short story of the Challenger), science fiction, sword and sorcery.

NEMESIS COMPANY series by Jeff Deischer
An homage to and pastiche of the Avenger, written in authentic pulp style.

*The Secret of the Suicidal Sparrow* (#1)
As the world becomes engulfed in war toward the end of 1941, Washington officials begin killing

themselves. The Basilisk is called in to investigare before the government is crippled.

*Red, as in Ruin* (#2)
It is 1942. America has just entered World War II. But other menaces threaten the citizens of the United States. Six years ago, tragedy took Simon Basil Petrie's family from him. From the ashes of his life as an inventor came the Basilisk, a being seemingly devoid of emotion devoted to one thing – battling crime and the weird criminals who perpetrate it. The Basilisk and his associates in Nemesis Company are summoned to Mexico when an old friend is attacked by a vampire, his body drained of blood!

*Sky Terror* (#3)
On their way back to New York City after a horrific case in Mexico, Nemesis Company is drawn into a strange adventure when their plane is stolen amidst a gun battle. Following the trail of a strange golden statuette of a bird, they discover a land that has been sealed off from the outer world for centuries.

*The World-Shakers* (#4)
When a mysterious force demolishes a house, and then another, Nemesis Company is summoned to investigate. What is doing the damage – and why?

*The Yesterday Menace* (#5)
When someone invents a working time machine, uit attracts the atention of prominent businessmen who see a way to make fortune – as do crooks. And Nemesis Company.

DOC BRAZEN series by Jeff Deischer
Ulysses "Doc" Brazen was a famous adventurer in the Thirties and Forties. An homage to and pastiche of Doc Savage.

*Millennium Bug* (#1)
A threat to his medical treatment of criminals brings Doc Brazen out of retirement, and, as he investigated, he collects a new batch of assistants. The mastermind behind the attack is Doc's equal.

*Dead Wrong* (#2)
Dead men return to life to assassinate all who pose a threat to their peace and contentment. Who is behind these strange murders – and why?

*Net Prophet* (#3)
When one of the Golden Man's aides is found in the most compromising of positions, he and his followers must investigate the strange murder of a young woman to clear him.

*Acid Test* (#4)
A mystery villain launches an all-out attack on the Golden Man's operation with a devastating new yet familiar weapon.

*Infernal Machine* (#5)
A devil visits New York City and decides he likes it. When Doc Brazen intervenes, he makes an enemy with seemingly supernatural powers.

*Golden Opportunity* (#6)
A woman's missing brother sends Doc Brazen and his aides to South America, where a white

god now rules a mountain tribe with an iron hand.

*Talking Heads* (#7)
Doc Brazen races to New Orleans to learn what happened to his missing aide, and finds a nest of zombies who used to be the wealthy elite of the Cresecent City.

*Element of Surprise* (#8)
When a criminal mastermind gains a secret wepaon that will give him control of the Atlantic Ocean, Doc Brazen is drawn into his web, leading to a msyterious island where untold treasure awaits.

*Wild Life* (#9)
The brutal murder of a friend takes Doc Brazen to an advanced science facility where things are not always what they seem. Among the employees hides a bestial murderer.

**Other Fiction**
"If You Can't Stand the Heat" by Jeff Deischer
Homage to a certain Sixties British spyfi TV program, updated for the Eighties. A retired secret agent and the daughter of his deceased partner team up to uncover the scheme of a madman who controls the weather. KINDLE ONLY

AGENT KEATS series by John Francis (Jeff Deischer)
An homage to and pastiche of James Bond, set in the Fifties, and written in Ian Fleming's style.

*Skull & Bones* (#1)
Mysterious Chinese coins are turning up in Hong Kong in 1952 amid ships disappearing in the area. John Sterling, agent Keats of the British Secret Service, is sent to find out the origin of the coins. Drawn into a web of shady characters such as Lemuel Gaunt, Malcolm Sweet and Mei Lei, Keats must determine where the coins are coming from and what happened to the previous agent sent to investigate.

*Chinese Puzzle* (#2)
John Sterling, agent Keats of the British Secret Service, is sent into Communist China in 1952 to learn what DRAGON is. What he knows is that DRAGON is an organization behind mysterious radio transmissions that resulted in the assassinations of several agents of Western Intelligence agencies. Is this a prelude to a deeper involvement by China in the Korean War? Or something more sinister?

*High Hopes* (#3)
John Sterling, Agent Keats of the British Secret Service, is sent to Greece to find out who's manufacturing Lovejoy, a synthetic LSD-type drug that been flooding the streets of London – and to put a stop to it. He soon finds himself between Charybdis and Scylla, two rival crime bosses as he searches for the mysterious drug lord behind.


A GOOD MAN series by Jeff Deischer
An homage to secret agent TV shows and spyfi, set at the end of the Seventies.

*A Good Man Returns* (#1)
Former secret agent Conrad Slade is called out of retirement when a mysterious criminal organization known as TAROT begins assassinating CIA agents.

*Revenge of the Radar Men*
A sequel to 1952 serial "The Radar Men from the Moon", the Radar Men return to menace Earth after the United Nations commandeered the lunar base.

*Partners in Crime*
In this traditional murder mystery set in 1946 Shanghai, newspaper reporter Percy Mitchell and his chanteuse wife Zhuang Xing investigate the murder of a family friend.

Printed in Great Britain
by Amazon